SAFE AS
HOUSES

SAFE AS HOUSES

a novel by ERIC WALTERS

SEAL BOOKS

Seal Books and colophon are trademarks of
Random House of Canada Limited.

SAFE AS HOUSES
Seal Books/published by arrangement with Doubleday Canada
Doubleday Canada edition published 2007
Seal Books edition published January 2009

ISBN 978-1-4000-2529-9

Cover design: Jennifer Lum

Seal Books are published by Random House of Canada Limited.
"Seal Books" and the portrayal of a seal are the property of
Random House of Canada Limited.

Visit Random House of Canada Limited's website:
www.randomhouse.ca

PRINTED AND BOUND IN THE USA

OPM   10   9   8   7   6   5   4

For Penny Doucette, who lived through the storm,
and Jim Crawford,
a genuine Canadian hero who saved her life.

TORONTO DAILY STAR

82ND YEAR

FRIDAY, OCTOBER 15, 1954—44 PAGES

5c PER COPY, 30c PER WEEK

THE WEATHER

'Hazel' Hurls Huge Waves
On U.S. Coast, Moves Inland

METRO EDITION

Fear Hurricane May Hit
Toronto Around Midnight

SAFE AS HOUSES

—

Suzie and I huddled beneath the umbrella. It gave us at least some protection from the rain that had been coming down in buckets all day. The whole school-yard was filled with kids bobbing about under umbrellas or in bright yellow slickers. A few of the boys from my Grade 8 class just turned up the collars of their denim jackets, like the rain wasn't any great inconvenience. They were too busy trying to look cool to even attempt to stay dry. Most of them were all wet even when it wasn't raining . . . although a few of them were cool even without the jacket. I looked around. I was waiting for Suzie's brother David, but I was hoping to catch sight of Donnie Davis. He was nowhere to be seen. Too bad.

Almost everybody was rushing to get away from the rain and home or to a friend's house. All my friends were going over to Debbie's to listen to some 45s on her new record player. Debbie had all the new songs—"Shake, Rattle and Roll" by Bill Haley, both versions of "Sh-Boom," by the Chords and by the Crew-Cuts, and "That's All Right" by Elvis Presley . . . Elvis was so dreamy . . . he would have been my favourite even if he couldn't sing.

I sighed. I hadn't even been invited. Everybody knew there was no point. I couldn't go, and asking me would have been cruel. Instead I was standing here, my saddle shoes soaked through, waiting. Couldn't David ever get here on time?

Suzie was pressed close against my leg, dressed in her little yellow raincoat and matching hat. It wouldn't have been nearly so dreadful if I were just babysitting *her* every night after school. She was a nice, sweet, friendly little Grade 2 kid. Nothing like her brother at all.

"How about if we just leave him here this time?" I asked.

Suzie giggled. We'd talked about this before. It was something we'd both have loved to do, but of course we couldn't. I was responsible for her brother as well, even if he didn't like it. I had to admit—at least to myself—that I understood why he felt he didn't need a sitter. He was in Grade 6 and should have been able to take care of himself. But his parents didn't trust him to watch out for Suzie, so I was in charge of both of them.

I looked at my watch—it was almost three-thirty. School had let out over ten minutes ago. That meant he wasn't just dawdling—he had a detention. David had to stay after class at least three times a week. Sometimes it was because he hadn't finished his work. Sometimes it was because of his behaviour. That boy just didn't like to be told what to do, and he loved to argue about why he shouldn't. I was tired of having those arguments with him. I could only imagine how much he must have annoyed the poor teacher who was stuck with him all day.

"Did he get in this much trouble at your old school?" I asked Suzie.

"Not as much," she replied.

They had moved to our neighbourhood this past summer. Mr. McBride had bought some land by the river. It seemed as though there were new houses going up there all the time. My father said they were "springing up like mushrooms." This was the third straight day of rain, so if what he was saying was true I guessed I could expect to see a dozen more there tomorrow.

Our house sat up on the hill overlooking the valley. I could see all those new houses from my bedroom window. Some seemed to go up all at once, started and finished in a few weeks. Others were ongoing projects, built little by little while the owners lived in them. That was the case with the McBrides' house. They had had the outside shell built for them—foundation, walls, roof, electrical, and plumbing—but then it was up to Mr. McBride to finish the inside. He was an accountant. I hoped he was better with numbers than he was with a hammer and saw because the work was going pretty slowly, and even I could tell that it wasn't being done particularly well.

"Here he comes," Suzie said.

David came out of the front doors. He didn't seem to be in any kind of hurry. He sort of swaggered toward us. He was carrying his school bag slung over one shoulder and he wasn't wearing a raincoat. I knew he had probably been sent to school in one this morning, so either he'd left it on a hook in his cubby or it was stuffed inside his bag. I could have asked him, but what was the point? It would only have led to an argument, and it wasn't as if I could physically force him to wear it.

"I'm not putting it on," he said defiantly, as if he were reading my mind.

Apparently he wanted an argument. Big surprise.

"Not putting on what?" I asked innocently.

"My raincoat. I have one, but I'm not going to wear it."

"What do I care?" I asked. "It's not me who's going to get soaked to the bone."

I took Suzie's hand and spun around, starting to walk away before he had a chance to react.

He scrambled to catch us. "My mother would want me to wear it."

"Then maybe you should."

"Are you telling me I have to?" he demanded.

"I'm not telling you anything."

"But you should," he argued. "That's your job, to make me do things that I don't want to do. You're the babysitter, aren't you supposed to make me do things, or at least *try* to make me do things?" He was really trying to get into it.

"They don't pay me enough to do that. Wear it or don't wear it. I don't care. Although your mother probably will when I tell her that you didn't wear it."

"You're going to tattle on me?"

"No, I'm not going to *tattle*. That would be so childish. I'm going to *report* to your mother. That's one of the things that babysitters do, tell the parents what their children did. She won't be happy."

"You'd better not tell her. She'll be just as mad at you for not making me put it on."

I shrugged. "Maybe she'll be so angry she'll even fire me."

"She might," he said smugly.

"And then she'll hire somebody else."

"Couldn't be anybody worse than the sitter we have."

"And you'd have a long, long time to learn to like her, because she'd probably be your sitter for the whole school year . . . maybe all of next summer."

"No way! We're only having a sitter until my birthday in January. Mom promised."

"She promised that it would only be to January *if* you proved you were responsible. Do you think it's responsible to have a detention after school, to not put on your raincoat, to fight with your sitter?"

He started to say something but stopped himself. I had him, and he knew it. He didn't want a babysitter now, but what he *really* didn't want was to put up with a sitter for any longer than necessary. The way out involved co-operating—unfortunately, not something that David was good at. At this rate, he might have a babysitter right through high school, and until he was married. Then his wife could be in charge.

David dropped back. I looked over my shoulder. He had put down his school bag and was pulling out his raincoat. I allowed myself a smile.

"I like having you as a babysitter," Suzie said.

"And I like being *your* babysitter."

We came to a stop at Weston Road. There were cars splashing along in both directions and we backed away from the road to avoid being sprayed. I squeezed Suzie's hand. We'd just wait for a big gap before we crossed and—David stepped onto the road! He dodged one car and then sprinted the rest of the way, reaching the safety of the sidewalk just before a truck rumbled by.

I waited for the light to change down the block at the corner so that our stretch of road would be free of traffic. Carefully I led Suzie across.

"You should be more careful of traffic," I warned him.

"You call this traffic?" he asked. "Traffic is what we have in Toronto, not up here in the *sticks*."

David was always making fun of Weston. He acted like it was a million miles north of the city instead of a thirty-minute car ride. I knew it wasn't the city, but it was a pretty big town and a really nice place to live. I liked Toronto, but I didn't really want to live there. I guess the way David didn't want to live here.

We turned onto my street, Hickory Tree Road. My house wasn't far ahead, just where the street curved, but we were heading to the McBride house, down the valley and across the Humber River. Their house was almost exactly twice as far from school as my house, a twenty-minute walk instead of just under ten. Twice as long was twelve times as miserable when the weather was like this. Thank goodness I wouldn't be walking with them all through the winter.

The road followed the lip of the valley, overlooking trees and grass and river. With all the rain, the Humber was brown and angry and wider than usual. It had burst its banks and was spreading out onto the flats. That wasn't so unusual during the spring floods, but it was strange to see it happen in the fall.

My house was just up ahead. I would have loved to have gone inside. I could have changed my clothes and dried my hair. Mom would have made me a snack and a hot cup of tea, or maybe hot chocolate. I knew I could have hot chocolate when we got to the McBrides' but it would be *me* fixing it for all of us. It always tasted better when somebody else made it. Actually, it tasted best when my mom made it.

I looked up. Mom was standing in the window. She was always there, each day, as we passed. I knew she was just worried—she was a worrier by nature—but it still felt as though she was spying on me, like she didn't trust me. It was embarrassing to have your mommy standing over you, watching and—she waved and smiled. I waved back weakly and gave her a little smile in return.

It was always such a strange thing to just walk past my house as though it didn't belong to me. I guess after six weeks I should have been getting used to it, but I wasn't. By January it might be different. Part of me would miss the money, but it would be nice to have my time back again. Time to spend with friends, or do my homework, or just not be responsible for two children. It was only a couple of hours each night, but sometimes the time really dragged. Funny how slowly time moves when you want to be someplace else.

This job sort of fell into my lap. My father runs a garage, and he had fixed Mr. McBride's car. He'd mentioned to my father that they needed a sitter every night for a couple of hours, from the time school dismissed until he and his wife arrived home, usually around six. It would only be for a few months, until David was older and able to look out for both himself and his sister. My father volunteered me, and when they offered me the job I jumped. I've always liked kids. I thought someday I might want to be a teacher. It was good to have my own money. I had my eye on a new record player like Donna's.

I had to walk them home from school, get them a snack, help Suzie with her homework, and, in the words of Mr. McBride, "try to stop David from doing anything too stupid." That last one was the real work. He was very creative in finding new and exciting ways to cause me trouble. After six weeks of taking care of him, I wasn't so sure I wanted to ever have children—at least not boys.

I also tried to straighten up the house a little every night. I'd wash the snack dishes, and the breakfast ones if they hadn't been done. In all the disorder of a house being constructed I needed to find some order. Once they'd had their snack and Suzie had done her homework, we'd sit on the chesterfield and turn on the television. The McBrides had the biggest television I had ever seen. Not that I'd seen too many—only a few of my friends had one—but their set was huge. It sat on the floor in a big, solid wooden cabinet with four legs. The screen had to be fifteen inches across, and the reception was so much better than on other sets. When the weather was good the picture was so clear that the faces were like you were looking right at the real person. If, that is, the real person was black and white and grey.

There was only one thing wrong with their television. Because their house sat at the bottom of the valley the only signal they could get was the CBC station from Toronto. They couldn't get either of the Buffalo stations which meant they didn't get any of the top American shows, as David constantly complained—another lousy thing about living in Weston. For me, one station was better than none, and that's what I got at home. We didn't have a television, and I didn't know if there was one in my immediate future.

While Mr. McBride hadn't yet attached the kitchen cupboards, he had just installed a big antenna on the roof of the house. Of course, true to form, he hadn't actually run a wire down and hooked it up to the television yet, but when he did he hoped to get those extra stations. But my father said that unless the antenna was higher than the sides of the valley he wouldn't be getting any new stations.

We got to a long set of wooden steps that led down the hill toward the river. They were wet and slick and slippery, and I held Suzie's hand even tighter. At the bottom we started along the gravel footpath. It was slightly elevated, and that rise put us above the surrounding grass, which was now more like a series of big puddles, so numerous and large that they were almost linking together into a shallow lake, an inch or so deep. There had been so much rain that it couldn't soak in or run off, it was just pooling up.

By the time we came to the footbridge that crossed the Humber the noise of the river had risen to a roar. The water raced by, brown and foamy and angry. Caught in its flow were tree branches, bobbing and bouncing along in the current. Some of the larger branches were now jammed into the underside of the bridge, trapping other garbage that had fallen in.

Suzie slowed down as we got closer to the river. She was always nervous around the bridge. She didn't like crossing it. Today I wasn't so crazy about it myself, even though it was a big, solid, wood-and-metal construction with high railings on the sides, anchored at both ends in gigantic concrete pilings. It was safe and secure, and there was nothing to worry about. My brain knew that. I just wished my stomach didn't have so many questions.

"So, what did you do in school today?" I asked Suzie as we started across, to take her mind off the rushing water below.

"We had a spelling bee, practising the words for the test on Monday."

"I hate spelling bees," I said.

Actually, what I really hated was the strange feeling in my stomach as the water rushed underneath our feet. I could just see it through the narrow cracks between the planks. It made me feel like I was being pushed sideways.

"I like spelling bees because I win a lot," Suzie said.

"Maybe that explains why *I* don't like them."

With each step toward the middle the roar of the water got louder, and Suzie's hold on my hand got stronger. For a little kid, she had one strong grip.

I couldn't help but watch the water. It was moving at an incredible clip. In the summer there were two or three spots where we went swimming. Just up from here was one of the best places. There was a curve in the river and it was deeper, calmer, and there was even a little sandy beach. Somebody had made a tire swing and you could swing out over the water and let go . . . of course that was just in the summer. Nobody was going to use that swing today. It was hard to believe this was even the same river.

I let out a silent little sigh as we reached the end of the bridge. It felt good to have my feet back on solid ground, even if some of it was a bit squishy. The river was so high that it had pushed up onto the shore, hit the concrete foundation, and swirled around into a little pool that had even washed away part of the gravel footpath.

I looked back and my heart did a flip. David was in the very middle of the bridge. He had climbed partway up the railing and his head and arms were hanging out over the river! He was just hanging there, dangling over the rushing water. What was he doing? Did he want to fall into the river? No, the railing was high enough that he couldn't actually fall . . . could he?

I started to yell at him but he couldn't hear me over the noise of the river. Or maybe he just wasn't listening.

"Wait here," I said to Suzie, handing her the umbrella.

I started back across the bridge. David was oblivious. He was leaning *way* over, balanced on the railing, staring down at the water. Was he looking at something, or was he just trying to make me crazy? I grabbed him by the arm and yanked him down.

"What are you doing?" he demanded.

"Getting you off the bridge. We have to get home," I said. "Suzie's soaking wet and I don't want her to catch cold." That sounded like a good excuse to get moving.

"But look down there," he said, pointing over the bridge.

"I've seen water before."

"No, look at the stuff jammed under the bridge."

Tentatively I leaned over. There among the branches were a broken lawn chair, a dented, crumpled garbage can, and a dead raccoon!

"Isn't that the biggest raccoon you ever saw in your life?" he questioned.

I shook my head in disgust.

"Look!" he exclaimed, pointing up the river now.

Caught in the brown water was a big, green picnic table. It was being whipped along, twisting and turning in the current, racing toward us. I watched as it got closer and closer and then it slammed into the garbage already trapped beneath the bridge.

"This is unbelievable!" David yelled over the roar. "I could watch this all day!"

"No, you can't," I argued. "We have to go."

I took a few steps and turned back around. He hadn't moved.

"Now!" I ordered, and to my surprise he followed me across the bridge.

"The water's higher than yesterday," David said.

"A lot higher. Higher than I've ever seen it," I admitted.

"Ever?"

"Ever."

"What will happen if it keeps raining?" he asked.

"Don't be such a goof. It'll stop. Maybe tonight."

"Or maybe after forty days and forty nights."

"Okay. If it keeps raining for that long you can build an ark and I'll start gathering pairs of animals."

"Har-de-har-har. You are *such* a comedian."

"Better to be funny-sounding than funny-looking," I said.

"Lucky you," he said. "You've managed both."

I decided it was best to ignore him. "Worst thing that will happen if it keeps raining is that your basement will flood. Wait, you don't have a basement, do you?"

"None of the houses on our street have basements."

That was right. The McBrides lived on Raymore Drive and I remembered my father telling me that the houses there were so close to the water table that if they'd tried to dig a basement more than a few feet deep they would have ended up digging a well instead. Besides, if they had built basements they would have just flooded every spring anyway. The river was high every spring, but it had never been this high in the fall.

Some of the houses sat on solid concrete foundations with bricks and blocks. With others, you could actually see right underneath the house because they were built on big wooden stilts that had been driven into the ground. I was starting to think that, before this rain was over, those people would be feeling pretty smart.

A few of the houses were big and sturdy looking, with paved driveways and beautiful flower gardens. Others were half finished or looked as if they'd been thrown together by a bunch of kids who had scrounged for lumber at the dump and borrowed their fathers' tools. Some didn't even have indoor toilets and had outhouses sitting out back.

David pulled out his house key. I always thought it was silly that the McBrides locked their door. Nobody else in Weston ever did. I guess it was different in the city. At the sound of the key in the door, Daisy, their dog, went crazy, barking and yelping. David opened the door slightly and we squeezed through. Daisy was jumping up and down and spinning in circles, and her little nub of a tail was wagging back and forth a mile a minute. She was always crazy-happy to see us—to see *them*—but I guess after being all alone for the entire day she might have been happy to see a burglar.

"Not so fast," I said to David as he started to kick off his shoes. "Daisy has to go out for a pee."

David shot me a dirty look but didn't argue. He knew walking the dog was one of his jobs. He grabbed a leash from a rack behind the door and clicked it onto Daisy's collar.

"And stay away from the river," I warned him.

"I won't be going anywhere near it."

I almost did a double take. Where was the smart aleck answer?

"This is the only springer spaniel in the world who's afraid of the water," he said. "I couldn't drag her near the river even if I wanted to."

"Just take her out to the front and I'll have hot chocolate waiting."

David went out with Daisy and Suzie went upstairs to change into some dry play clothes. I couldn't change, but at least I could get out of some of my wet things. I hung up my rain jacket and removed my shoes and bobby socks. I wrung the socks out as much as I could in the kitchen sink and hung them on one of the coat hooks behind the door, but water still dripped onto the plywood floor. I turned the shoes over and leaned them against the wall.

I padded across the floor, carefully lifting my feet to avoid picking up any slivers. When was Mr. McBride going to finish the floor . . . or finish anything? If this house was a work in progress, there was very little progress being made. The kitchen was no more finished than the rest of the house. He'd hung cupboards on the wall, but they were slightly crooked and didn't have doors. That certainly made it easy to see where everything was, but it didn't add to any sense of order.

I ran water into the kettle and placed it on the stove. I got down a box of Oreos and put them out on a plate. I took one and popped it in my mouth. I heard the front door open and then close. That didn't take long.

"It's raining harder," David yelled out.

I poked my head out of the kitchen. "At least we have the tools and wood to build that ark," I said, pointing to a pile of lumber in the corner of the living room.

The materials that were going to be needed to finish the house were lying around everywhere. Panelling, doors for the kitchen cupboards, flooring, and tools were piled around the house. It would have driven me crazy to live like that.

The phone rang, startling me.

"I'll get it!" Suzie yelled from the stairs, racing down, two at a time.

I was closer to the phone but she wanted to answer it, because we both knew who was on the other end of the line.

She ran in and grabbed the phone. "Hello, Mommy!" she sang out.

Mrs. McBride called home every day. I think she needed to know that we were safely in the house, but she also probably missed the kids and the routine of being with them. Before she'd gone to work with her husband in the new accounting business he'd started, *she* would have met them at the school and been the one to walk them home and fix them hot chocolate.

Suzie was answering questions about her day— the same questions my mother always asked. I think my mother missed me coming straight home to tell her how my day had gone. Not that I told her very much. There were things a thirteen-year-old girl would *never* tell her mother.

"Here," Suzie said, handing me the phone.

"Hello, Mrs. McBride."

"Hello, Elizabeth. Is everything well?"

The line was filled with static and her voice sounded very far away.

"Fine. Everything is good."

"I called a few minutes ago," she said.

"We were a bit late leaving school."

There was no point in telling her why. That was between her, the school, and David.

"It's raining very hard here in Toronto," she said. "How is it there?"

I looked through the front window. It was raining so hard that I could barely see the houses across the street.

"It's coming down pretty heavy here, too."

"My husband is with a client right now. As soon as he's finished I'm going to convince him that we should leave right away."

"So you might be home early?" I asked hopefully.

"We might leave early, but we might arrive late. You know how city traffic can get snarled in the rain."

"Yes," I agreed, although I didn't really know. My trips to Toronto had been limited to the occasional Sunday morning.

"If we're not there by six, do you think you could start supper?"

"I could just start it anyway," I offered.

"That's so kind of you. After getting up early, driving to the city, working all day, and then driving home, it's sometimes hard to find the energy to make a decent meal. It would be such a pleasure to have things started when I walked in the door."

"It's no problem."

"There's leftover meatloaf in the refrigerator that could be warmed up. And if you could boil some potatoes . . . they're under the sink."

The kettle started whistling.

"Do you want to talk to David?"

"You just say hello for me and I'll see him when we get home."

"See you when you get here," I said.

"Bye, Mommy!" Suzie yelled out as I started to hang up.

"Let's make that hot chocolate," I said.

David had changed and was already planted on the chesterfield in front of the television. Suzie followed me into the kitchen. I took the kettle off the burner and instantly the annoying whistling changed tone and then faded away. I hated having a kettle order me about like that.

I poured the boiling water into three cups and Suzie came over with a spoon and the hot chocolate mix.

"Somehow it doesn't seem fair that we're making the hot chocolate and David gets to just sit there and watch television," I said.

"That's what Mommy says about Daddy sometimes."

"Well *my* husband had better not expect to be waited on hand and foot."

"You have a husband?" Suzie gasped.

I laughed. "I'm only thirteen. But when I *do* have a husband he'd better help out. I'm going to be a wife, not a servant."

"Me neither!" Suzie agreed. "I'm not going to be a servant!"

"Good for you!"

She picked up one of the mugs. "I'll bring this in for my brother."

Not a good start.

The rain was pounding against the window above the sink. I picked up the mug and went over and peered through the glass. I could hardly see the garden shed and woodpile that sat at the end of their yard, by the river. I could just barely make out the river, overflowing the banks and washing up onto the grass. I hoped they didn't have anything in that shed that shouldn't get wet. Not the brightest place to put a shed, right by the river.

I heard David complaining from the other room. I walked in. He was fiddling with the little rabbit-ear antenna, trying to improve the reception.

"Stupid television," he grumbled.

"There, that's better," I called out.

Not wonderful but certainly better than it had been. It was a kids' show featuring a bunch of puppets. I settled into the chesterfield beside Suzie. She snuggled in and I wrapped an arm around her as she giggled. Funny, I was far too old to watch a puppet show, but watching it on television seemed to make it okay.

"The reception is so much better in the city," David said.

"Isn't *everything* better in the city?" I asked.

"That's right. Everything. I wish we'd never moved here."

I knew that there was probably one teacher and definitely one babysitter who thought the same thing.

"As soon as I'm old enough I'm going to move back."

"Nice plan. Before you move out, you might want to try not having a babysitter."

He scowled, but didn't say anything. Instead he got up and started to fiddle with the rabbit ears again. It got worse and then better again. He slumped back into his seat.

I liked television. It wasn't that any of the shows were particularly good, but it was like my Nana used to say: it isn't that a dancing bear dances well, just that it dances at all. It was pretty amazing to sit there and have all those people and things come right into your living room to entertain you.

I'd heard from some of my friends about shows that had singers and movie stars, but I'd never seen any of them. I would have *loved* to see Bill Haley and The Comets, or Elvis. Boy would I have liked to see Elvis. Even better, to see *and* hear the Penguins perform "Earth Angel." I would have died for that.

I started humming to myself, ". . . will you be mine . . . mmm-mm . . . darling dear . . ."

"You should save your voice," David said. "Maybe for Donnie."

"Donnie Davis?"

"Unless you're in love with another Donnie."

"I don't even know another Donnie."

"Then that's the one you're in love with," he said.

"I'm *not* in love with him." I was trying to sound casual and convincing all at once.

"Then I guess everybody is wrong."

Everybody? What did he mean by everybody? I felt myself blush at the same time my stomach did a little flip. Did everybody really know how I felt? Did Donnie know?

"I don't even like him."

"I'll be sure to tell him that the next time I see him. You know, so nobody else gets the wrong impression."

"Don't you dare tell him that—" I stopped myself, feeling trapped. "It's just that it wouldn't be nice to tell him that. Besides, it's not that I don't like him, I just don't like him *that* way. When does the news come on?" I asked, trying to change the subject.

"You hoping the news will report that you don't like Donnie *that way*?" David taunted.

"Maybe the news will report that an annoying boy was beaten up by his babysitter."

"As if."

I could see him bristling for a fight. I decided it was beneath me to fight with the kid I was babysitting.

"I want to see what they have to say about the weather."

"I could be wrong," David said, "but I think they're going to tell you that it's raining."

"And you think *I'm* a comedian. I want to know how long it's going to keep on raining. When is the news on?"

"Soon. At six."

"Your parents will be home before that."

"We can hope," he said.

I'd already cleaned up the kitchen, set the table for supper, and peeled the potatoes when the phone rang again.

"Hello, Elizabeth."

My heart sank. It was Mrs. McBride. Nobody ever calls to say they are going to be on time.

"We're going to be late," she said, confirming my fears. "We've been on the road since just after four." It was a terrible connection. Her voice was crackly and tinny.

"But it's after five-thirty now."

"The roads are just terrible. I had my husband stop at a phone booth so I could let you know. The rain has flooded out some roads completely, and there are underpasses where the water is so deep cars are stalling out. The wind has taken down trees and wires. The whole city is a mess. The traffic lights aren't working at some intersections. You have power, right?"

"Power? Oh, yes, we have electricity." I hadn't even thought of that possibility. What would I do with two kids in a house without power? How would I even finish making supper?

"Elizabeth, I know it's an imposition, but we really need you to stay with the children."

"Of course. I wouldn't dream of leaving them alone."

"If they were a little older it wouldn't be so bad just for an hour or so. I can't imagine it will take us any longer than that."

"That's okay, Mrs. McBride. I'll feed them supper."

"Thank you so much. You should call your mother and let her know what's happening. I'm sure she's worried, and she'll get more worried when you're late."

"I'll call as soon as we hang up."

"And tell her my husband will drive you home. Nobody should be out on a night like this."

"It's not far for me to walk," I said without thinking. Then I realized it would be late and dark and pouring rain. And I would have to cross the river by myself on that little footbridge.

"No, we insist."

"Thank you," I said, relieved. "There'll be plates in the oven waiting for you and Mr. McBride, and I'll put on a pot of coffee."

"Elizabeth, you are a lifesaver. It's so good to know that the children are in such good hands."

"They're as safe as houses."

Mrs. McBride laughed. "My mother used to say that all the time."

"So did my Nana," I said. "Although I'm not even sure what it means."

"I've always thought it meant that you're never as safe, anywhere, as you are in your own house."

This wasn't my house, but we were safe here. The worst thing that could happen would be the electricity going out. Sitting in the dark without a television to keep David happy would be hard, but not impossible.

"Just so you know, if the power goes off there are candles—"

"In the cupboard above the fridge," I said.

"I guess that's an advantage to not having doors on the cupboards. And, of course, we'll pay you for staying later."

"That's not necessary," I said. "This is just what neighbours do."

"Everyone is so friendly in Weston."

"I guess we all know each other here."

"Well, I just know that you're a doll, Elizabeth. Oh, my husband is honking at me. I'd better go. The sooner we get going the sooner we'll get there."

"Drive carefully . . . bye."

I put the phone down. The second it settled into the cradle it rang again, and I shrieked in surprise. David turned away from the television and gave me a look like I was a complete idiot. Which was how I felt.

"It startled me," I tried to explain. I picked it up. "Hello?"

"Hello, Lizzy."

It was my mother. The line was filled with static, no better than when I was talking to Mrs. McBride.

"I've been trying to reach you."

"I was talking to Mrs. McBride."

"I was hoping that you were talking to somebody. When the lines go down it gives a busy signal and I was afraid that your phone was out. There are lines down across the city."

"Mrs. McBride told me. They're running a bit late."

She sighed. "I was hoping they'd be there soon."

"They left early but she said the roads are terrible, traffic lights aren't working, power lines are down, roads are flooded."

"Your father just called and said the same thing," she told me. "He's out with his tow truck. There are stalled cars all over the city. He's even had to fish a car out of a flooded underpass. He told me the man was sitting on the roof of his car, like it was a little island."

That struck me as funny and I laughed. My mother chuckled at the other end of the line.

"Did Mrs. McBride say how long they thought they might be?" my mother asked.

"They didn't know, but they weren't even close. They said they'd try to get here as soon as possible. I'm going to fix supper for the children."

"That's a good idea. Now, Lizzy, this is important. When they do arrive home, under no circumstances are you to try to use the footbridge to come home on."

"Mr. McBride is going to drive me."

"It might be better if your father came and got you in the truck. Raymore Drive must be a canal by now.

Unless you hear differently from me, you should expect him to come and get you around nine."

"But that's not for over three hours!" It already seemed like I'd been here too long.

"It might take them that long to get home. Call when they get there, okay? If your father is free sooner he'll come and wait with you until the McBrides arrive."

"Okay, thanks, that would be good."

"You'll be fine, Lizzie." I guess she had heard the uneasiness in my voice. "Just sit tight, stay inside and dry. Watch some television with the children, and remember, you're as safe as houses."

That made me smile.

"I know. I'll call when they get home."

"And try to stay off the line until then. Never wise to be on the phone during an electrical storm."

"It's not going to hit the phone line, Mom," I said.

"You know how I worry."

"*That* I know," I said.

"I love you, Lizzie. Bye for now."

I hung up the phone. There was no point in feeling sad about the whole thing. There was work to do. I might as well start boiling the potatoes. A good, warm, filling meal would be the ticket to feeling better. At least if the power went out supper would be cooked. I walked into the kitchen, put a lid on the pot, and turned on the burner.

A flash of lightning suddenly illuminated the whole sky, followed almost immediately by a clap of thunder. That meant the storm was practically on top of us. I looked out the window. It wasn't that late. There should still have been some light, but the thick clouds and heavy rain had made night come early. There was another burst of lightning and the world was lit up again. Up the river I could just make out the outline of the footbridge. I could see the skeleton of the railings and—wait, that couldn't be right. Then a third flash of lightning, and what I saw astonished me. The water was bouncing against the side of the bridge and flooding right over it! The railings were still clearly above the water, but there was water going *over* the bridge. I'd never seen *that* before, even during the spring floods. It would have been impossible to walk across the bridge now. Thank goodness I was going to be getting a drive instead.

I just stood there at the window watching the rain pound down, waiting for another lightning burst to illuminate the scene. I was as fascinated by the weather as David was by the television. It was a phenomenal storm.

One more gigantic flash lit up the whole sky, the whole room, and then it went dark everywhere. The lights in the house had gone off. The television had gone off. For a few seconds nobody said anything; the only sound was the rain pounding against the windows. Then there was another flash of lightning that lit up the room eerily. In that split second I saw Suzie standing in the doorway to the kitchen. She looked panic-stricken. I tried to think of something to say to reassure her, but before I could come up with anything the lights flickered and came on, then went off, then, thank heavens, came back on again to stay.

I walked toward Suzie. "See, there's nothing to worry about," I said cheerfully, trying to reassure her.

"I wasn't worried," David called out from the living room. He sounded almost angry. "Just annoyed that the television went off."

"Sometimes the power goes off for a few seconds when there's lightning," I continued, ignoring him.

David stood up and turned the set back on. A little greyish light started to glow in the middle of the screen. It got lighter and whiter and slowly grew until it took up the whole screen. The white resolved into different shades until fuzzy figures appeared.

"Maybe you should do your homework instead of watching television," I suggested.

"Why should I?" he asked. "I've got all weekend."

"Isn't it better to do your homework on Friday night so you have the rest of the weekend to just enjoy yourself?" I suggested.

"I think I'm going to wait and see what happens. The way it's raining, there's a chance there won't be any school on Monday."

"What do you think is going to happen? Do you think the school is going to float away?" I asked.

"I can hope."

"Better not hope too hard. Think about it. The school is up on the hill, and we're down here by the river. If the school floated away, what do you think would happen to us?"

"*Could* something happen to us?" Suzie asked. She sounded anxious.

"Nothing will happen to us," I said firmly, kicking myself for having spooked her. "We're in a house. Houses don't float away." I turned to David. "Schools don't float away. Even if the lights go out again, all that means is that we'll be safe in the dark instead of safe in the light."

"I don't like the dark," Suzie said.

"Neither do I. Let's make sure it doesn't get dark, even if the lights do go out again. Come." I took Suzie's hand and led her into the kitchen. Daisy followed along behind us, her toenails click-clicking on the plywood floor until she stopped at her empty bowl and looked up. I was temped to add some more food to her bowl, just to make her happy, but I'd been told not to do that. Apparently Daisy would just keep eating and eating and eating. Maybe she didn't like water but she did like food. Daisy was one pudgy dog.

I pushed over a chair, climbed up, reached up over the fridge, and pulled down the candles. There were five. Two were just little stubs and three had never been lit.

"Can you get me five egg cups?" I asked.

Suzie climbed up on another chair and so she could reach the cupboard. I pulled a roll of aluminum foil out of a drawer. Suzie put the egg cups on the counter, I ripped off a piece of foil and rolled it around the end of a candle, then put it snuggly in the egg cup so it would stand up. I repeated the process four more times.

"If the lights go out, we're ready," I said.

"Could we light one of them now?" Suzie asked.

"Why not? I'll just . . ." I didn't have matches, and I didn't even know where to look.

"I know where there are matches," Suzie said, without me even asking. She ran quickly out of the room, and when she returned I lit one candle and set it on the counter, out of the way.

"Do you think Mommy and Daddy will be here soon?" Suzie asked.

"Could be soon."

"But it could be longer, right?"

I shook my head. "It's almost six-thirty. They left at four. They could practically walk here in three hours."

Suzie's face brightened.

"Don't worry," I said. "It's just rain. It's not like they're made of gingerbread—they won't melt. I bet you they'll be home by the time we eat supper. Why don't you wash your hands and help me put the food out."

I finished washing the last of the supper dishes and went back to join the kids in the living room. It was starting to look as if the McBrides *had* melted. Where were they? They could have at least called to let me know where they were and when they would get here.

I was happy that Suzie had drifted off. She and Daisy were all snuggled up together in a little ball on the floor, looking like a picture in a calendar. David sat, stone still, on the chesterfield, watching the television. He'd given up trying to improve the reception. The picture was fuzzy, flashing and rolling and fading, and the sound cracked and popped. I would have told him to turn it off long ago if it hadn't been for the weather updates. Some of the news was reassuring. They were predicting that the rain would stop sometime during the night. We were getting the tail end of a hurricane—they called it Hurricane Hazel—that had hit way down south in the United States. Thank goodness we weren't down there, where the hurricane could do real damage.

However, most of what was reported was just disturbing. The roads were a mess of accidents, stalled cars, downed hydro wires, and fallen trees.

Power was out in large parts of the city and phones weren't working in some areas. I'd jumped up a couple of times to pick up the receiver, just to make sure there was still a dial tone. It was amazing how comforting that buzzing sound was.

One time the announcer said that the downtown hotels were filling up with people unable to drive home. I was sure that wasn't the case with Mr. and Mrs. McBride, though. They were taking a long time but they were still coming, I was positive.

I wondered what would happen if my father got here first. I'd even thought about just tucking the kids into bed and leaving with him, but I knew there was no way I could do that, no matter how much I wanted to go home. My father would just wait—unless we *all* went back to our house. We could do that. There was certainly room in the truck for all of us. We could even bring Daisy. Poor dog would have to get wet getting to the truck, but we couldn't leave her alone, either. I would just leave the McBrides a note telling them where we were.

I walked over to the front window and peered out into the darkness once again. Occasionally lights would appear on the edge of the valley—cars moving along the road. At least *somebody* was moving. And I could hope that the next set of lights might turn down the road and come toward us and that it would be Mr. and Mrs. McBride. Or even better, my father. I could just picture his tow truck splashing through the street, turning into the driveway, my father jumping out of the cab wearing his big black slicker and running up to the house and deciding what we all needed to do.

"Do you think we should move her upstairs?" David asked.

"What?" I turned away from the window.

He pointed to Suzie. "Do you think we should try to move her upstairs?"

"Let her sleep until your parents get home. As long as she's asleep she isn't worried," I said. "Are you worried?"

"Yeah, right, like I'm afraid of some rain."

"It's a whole lot of rain."

"That's just a whole lot of nothing to worry about. Are *you* worried?" he asked.

I didn't answer. I didn't want to lie.

He snorted. "Why don't you roll into a little ball with Suzie and Daisy and you can go to sleep and I'll babysit everybody."

"I'm not worried."

"You're looking and acting worried." He was pushing me again, looking for an argument. Why didn't he just go back to watching the television and ignoring me.

"I'm just concerned about your parents. Aren't you?"

It was David's turn to be silent. Now I'd made him uneasy. What a great babysitter I was, scaring the kids instead of reassuring them.

"I'm sure they'll be home soon," I said quickly. "Until they get here, we'll just watch television. Do you want me to get you something else to eat?" He hadn't eaten much supper.

"Thanks . . . that would be nice."

It seemed like the least I could do after what I'd said. I walked into the kitchen and had just opened the fridge when suddenly the lights went out again and I was standing in semi-darkness. The little candle in the egg cup was still sitting on the counter, and the light that had seemed so weak and faint was now strong and warm and welcoming.

"The lights will be back on soon," I said, loudly enough for David to hear. "Please come back on," I pleaded quietly, under my breath. I started counting. I reached ten. Still no lights. I lit a second candle and walked back to the living room, careful not to let it go out.

"Do phones work in the dark?" David asked.

"Why wouldn't they? You can talk in the dark."

"You don't need electricity to talk. Do phones work when there's no power?" he asked.

I didn't know . . . I'd never even thought about it. I grabbed the phone out of the cradle and put it up to my ear. Instant relief. "It's working, there's a dial tone."

"That just means that it has a dial tone. Call somebody. Why don't you call Donnie and tell him you don't like him *like that*."

I wanted to tell him to shut up. Instead I started to dial. I knew who I wanted to talk to. There was a brief hesitation after I dialed the seventh number and then it started to ring. It was picked up immediately.

"Hello?"

"It's me, Mom."

"Oh, Lizzie, I was just talking to your father. His truck has stalled." She sounded worried.

"But how is he going to pick me up?" Now *I* was getting worried.

"You'll have to stay there tonight."

"Mrs. McBride said that Mr. McBride would drive me home."

"Given how your father has described the roads, I think there's a very good chance that they won't be able to reach you tonight."

"But wouldn't they have called if they weren't coming home?"

"Maybe they can't get to a phone that's working. Phones and power are out in places across the city. My electricity just went out again a few minutes ago. Do you still have power?"

"It just went out."

"Do you have candles or flashlights?" she asked.

"Candles. I have a couple burning now."

"Be careful with the flames. Make sure you blow them out before you go to bed tonight."

"Mom, I'm not a kid." But despite those words it suddenly sank in. I was sleeping here, maybe with just the kids, me watching, being in charge.

"I know, Lizzie, but you'll always be *my* kid. I want you to call me if you hear from the McBrides or if they get home."

"I'll call right away."

"And call me once or twice before you go to bed. We'll just hope the phones continue to work. They're calling Hurricane Hazel the storm of the century, and the phones might go down, the way the electricity did."

It felt as if there were butterflies in my stomach.

"Lizzie, I wish you were right here beside me."

Not nearly as much as I wished that same thing, no matter how confident I was trying to sound.

"But I'm so glad for the sake of those children that you're right there," she went on. "Can you imagine how terrible it would be for them to be there by themselves?"

I looked over at Suzie, sleeping, snuggled in with Daisy. David wouldn't admit it, but he needed me to be there, too.

"And, Lizzie, I love you."

"I love you, too. I'll talk to you soon."

I put the phone down and took a deep breath, trying to chase away the butterflies. I didn't want to sleep here tonight. I didn't even want to *be* here right now. I peered through the window. If there had been a bit more light, and I'd looked hard enough, I might have actually made out a couple of houses on my street. So close and yet so far.

Maybe I couldn't get to my bed, but it was time to get Suzie into hers. She was still sleeping peacefully on the floor. Gently I lifted her up. Her head flopped to the side but she didn't wake up.

"David," I said, softly. "Can you take one of the candles and lead the way, please?"

"How about if I do this instead."

A beam of light shot out, illuminating the entire staircase.

"You have a flashlight!"

"No, I have *two* flashlights." A second beam shot straight into my eyes, blinding me until I turned my head. He turned it off.

"Why didn't you tell me you had flashlights?"

"You seemed to like the candles. Besides, I didn't want to waste the batteries."

"Help me upstairs."

David led the way and trailed the light behind him so I could see the stairs. Suzie wasn't big but she was a dead weight and I struggled as I climbed, being careful not to trip. Her room was right at the top of the stairs. David pulled back the bed covers and I laid her down and tucked her in. She was still in her clothes, but I didn't want to wake her.

Her eyes opened ever so slightly.

"It's bedtime . . . go to sleep," I whispered.

"Goodnight, Elizabeth." Her eyes closed again.

I gave her a little kiss on the cheek. As I stood up, Daisy jumped up onto the end of the bed. She made a little circle and then settled in. I scratched her behind the ears. Then David handed me a flashlight and we tiptoed back downstairs.

We both walked over to the front window and looked out. I knew he was feeling worried—we were both worried—but neither of us wanted to talk about it.

"Do you think it's slowing down?" he asked.

"I'm almost afraid to say it, but I think it is."

"The last news flash before the electricity went out said it was supposed to slow down or even stop, maybe even before midnight. What time is it?"

I turned on the flashlight so I could see my wristwatch. "It's almost ten."

"I've never seen rain like this," David said.

"Not just today. It's rained every day for the last ten days, and non-stop for the last three."

"I guess that's why it's slowing down," David said. "No more rain left to fall."

"I'm glad the lightning has stopped."

"Not me. At least we got little bursts of light to see what was happening outside. Now it's just dark." He looked over at me. "Do you think my parents are going to make it home tonight?"

"I'm sure they're still trying. It's pretty rough out there."

"I think they should stop trying," he said. "It might be better if they just stayed put and waited out the storm."

I hadn't expected him to say that. I thought he'd want them home and me gone.

"We'll be okay," David said. "There are worse things than not having electricity. This is sort of like camping, that's all."

"I guess you're right," I admitted.

We stood side by side looking out the window into the darkness. Occasionally car headlights would briefly appear up on the side of the valley. It was reassuring to know that some vehicles were still on the road.

"You know, I don't need a babysitter."

"What?"

"I don't need a babysitter."

I couldn't believe he was going into this again, now, with everything else that was going on. If he was being so stubborn and stupid maybe I should just leave him here right here and now . . . of course, I couldn't do that.

"I just wanted you to know that."

There was no point in getting into a fight, no matter how much he wanted to. I guess without television he needed something to pass the time. I wasn't going to play his game.

"Actually, I'm going to tell your parents how good you've been through this."

"You are?"

"Look, David, I know you could take care of yourself and Suzie."

"You just figuring that out *now*?" he asked.

Again I decided I wasn't going to fight. I didn't say a thing.

"But you know," he said, "I'm glad you're here."

That surprised me. No, that *shocked* me. Had I heard him wrong?

"It's good, you know, for Suzie. I think it makes her feel better." Then, after a pause, he asked, "Where are you going to sleep tonight?"

"I hadn't really thought about it. Maybe here on the chesterfield."

"It's not very comfortable. You can have my room if you want, and I'll sleep down here," David offered.

"Thanks, David, but I don't want to put you out. Besides, when your parents get home it'll be easier this way . . . in case your father wants to drive me home." I hadn't given up that thought completely.

"Okay, but let me know if you change your mind."

"Thanks. What about Daisy?" I asked. "Doesn't she have to go out one more time?"

"Yeah, usually my father takes her out before he goes to bed."

"That's what I thought. How about you bring Daisy down and get her leash on and I'll brave the storm?" I suggested.

David went upstairs. I took my socks down from the coat hook. They were still damp. I hung them back up and slipped into my saddle shoes, which were also still wet. Then I slipped on my damp, cold raincoat. I shivered, dreading getting soaked again.

David was dragging Daisy down the stairs by her collar. She definitely did not want to leave Suzie and her warm bed, and she probably knew what this was leading to. He took down her leash and clicked it on.

"I won't go too far," I said.

"Daisy won't *let* you go too far."

I took her leash and started to open the door. It was wrenched out of my hand and almost caught me in the side of the head. The wind was incredibly strong and the rain was being driven almost horizontally. I struggled to pull Daisy through the doorway. She dug in her heels and it was a battle, pulling her, pushing through the wind and fighting against the driving rain.

"I'll get the door!" David yelled over the noise of the wind and rain. He put his shoulder to the door and closed it behind us.

The rain was like hundreds of painful little pellets stinging my face. I turned my head but there was no escape. The rain seemed to be coming from every side. I stepped off the porch and into a puddle deeper than my shoes. I sloshed forward another step. Now both feet were ankle deep in water. It wasn't a puddle, it was a pond, a lake. The whole front yard was under water!

I towed Daisy down the drive, through the water, and to the street, dipping my head, and bending over to fight my way through the wind. Raymore wasn't a road any more, it was a river! It was almost dark but it didn't matter, I could hear the water rushing down the street. In the faint light I could see objects moving in the water . . . a piece of wood . . . a flattened lawn chair . . . a garbage can lid, spinning around, caught in the current. Unbelievable.

If I stepped onto the road I would be stepping *into* a river about half a foot deep. Would the current knock me off my feet, carry me away like another piece of debris? My heart sank as I realized there was no way a car would be coming down this street any time soon. We were cut off from the world by the flowing river of Raymore.

I looked down at Daisy. She was a pudgy little anchor holding me in place, little legs practically lost beneath the water. She looked miserable. There was no way she was going to pee in this torrent. There was no point in even being out here. I turned back toward the house and she surged forward, towing me along this time. She wanted to get back to the house even more than I did.

We climbed the steps, out of the freezing water, onto the porch. I knew we should just go inside, but there was something about standing out there and letting the storm hit me full force. Inside, even though I could see the rain, hear it against the windows and roof, it wasn't the same. Out here, with it stinging my face, my feet soaked, the sounds not filtered through the walls of the house, it was completely *real*. That should have made it more scary, but somehow it didn't. We'd handled the worst that the storm could dish out and we were still standing. It could take away the electricity, but it couldn't get inside the house and harm us. It might be dark, but it was dry. We were safe. Safe as houses.

Daisy tugged at the leash and pawed at the door, whining. Obviously she wasn't enjoying this moment the way I was. I opened the door, and the force of the wind combined with Daisy propelled me through. I dropped the leash and then pushed hard against the door to close it. Finally I peeled off my jacket and kicked off my soaked shoes. I didn't even want to think what all this water was doing to them.

"Here," David said. He was standing on the stairs in his pyjamas. He threw down a blanket and I caught it.

"What's it like out there?" he asked.

"I think the rain is slowing down." I didn't really know, but I liked to think that it was a little bit lighter. "But the wind is still really strong." I wondered whether I should tell him the next part, but I figured I needed to share it. "The whole street is flooded. I don't think there's any way your parents can get here tonight."

He nodded his head. "That's what I figured." He paused. "That's okay. You sure you don't want to sleep in my bed instead of down here?"

"I'll be okay. See you in the morning."

"Okay. Good night." He retreated back up the stairs.

Funny, David's attitude seemed to get better as the situation got tougher. That was at least something to be grateful for. Maybe after I told his parents how he handled himself calmly and responsibly through this, they might agree he really could take care of Suzie and himself. I'd be out of a job, but really, five days a week was a bit much, especially when one of those nights was as long as this one.

I went to spread out the blanket on the chesterfield and lie down, but I remembered I had to blow out the candle still burning in the kitchen. I blew it out, and the room became darker with just the candle in the living room still glowing.

The rain came down hard, like a sheet, hitting against the kitchen window. I walked over and put my hands against the glass to try to peer out, but there was nothing but black. Suddenly the world was illuminated by a series of lightning strikes, one after the other. I could see the river. It had exploded from its banks and was cutting through the back of the yard, through the place where the shed and woodpile had once sat. They were gone. A shiver went up my spine. The road was like a river on one side of the house, and the river was rising on the other. It was as if we were on a little island. An island was a safe place to be. Wasn't it? I wished my parents were here—then I thought about the promise I'd made to call my mother.

I went back to the living room and picked up the phone. No dial tone. Not a sound. No hum. Nothing. The phone was dead.

It felt like being on a ship, on a stormy sea. We had no power, no electricity, and now, without the telephone, we had no way to call back to shore. We were alone. And I was the captain.

I pulled the blanket up and flipped over, trying to find some way to get comfortable. I should have taken David up on his offer. His bed had to be more comfortable than this. Sleeping on a bed of *nails* would have been more comfortable than this.

I closed my eyes tightly, trying to will myself to sleep. I'd woken up time and time again, tossing and turning and worrying. It was hard to sleep in a strange place at the best of times, and this was not the best of times. My eyes would open, and in the darkness I'd try to figure out where I was. It would take a few seconds. Strange bed, strange house, strange sounds. The sound of water.

My head was filled with images of water. Rain, the raging river, the flooded roads. Things I'd seen, but also images of things I'd heard about. Flooded underpasses, cars stalled out, downed wires, my father in his black slicker in his tow truck, the McBrides trying to get home. Not tonight. No one was getting here tonight.

I didn't know what time it was. It might have been midnight, but it might have been two in the morning. I tried to look at my wristwatch but it was too dark. The flashlight. Where was it . . . ? Oh yeah, I'd put it on the end table in the corner. I threw my feet off the chesterfield and they splashed into freezing cold water! I screamed at the shock and jumped up at the same time. There was water halfway up my calves!

I sloshed over to the table, grabbed the flashlight, and turned it on. I swept the light around the room. There was water everywhere! The whole house was flooded with a foot of water! There were things—a doll Suzie had left on the floor, a slipper, pieces of wood, a kitchen cupboard door—floating through the room! I took a few steps toward the front door, water splashing up as I walked, then stopped and turned toward the phone. I had to call my father—he'd know what to do. I stopped. Of course I couldn't call him, the line was dead. Regardless, I picked up the phone, praying for a dial tone. Silence.

I heard a noise behind me and turned. David was standing on the stairs in his pyjamas, shining a beam of light across the floor. What *used* to be the floor. I splashed over and climbed the stairs and stood beside him.

"Oh my God," he whispered. "It's . . . it's everywhere."

He let the flashlight play around the living room. It was strangely reassuring to know that somebody else was seeing the same thing I saw. A second set of eyes witnessing it made it seem real, not some sort of strange dream.

"The television!" David suddenly yelled.

He pushed by me and jumped, landing in the water with a tremendous splash.

"What are you doing?" I screamed. "Get back up here. Are you crazy?"

"The television! We have to save the television! The water is still below the tubes. We can save it if we move it right now! You have to help me lift it up!" he yelled.

I looked at him. He was standing in over a foot of water, *inside* his house, getting ready to lift the television.

"That's crazy, David! We have to think about—"

"What will my parents think when you could have helped save the television, but you didn't? It's worth a lot of money. Help me!" he pleaded.

He sounded so desperate and genuine. Besides, what was it that I thought we should do instead? I stumbled over, icy water splashing up my legs.

"Lift up that side," he ordered. "We'll put it on the kitchen table."

I turned off my flashlight and slipped it into the pocket of my skirt.

He placed his flashlight, still on, on top of the television. "And be careful when we move it. We have to keep it flat so the flashlight doesn't roll off."

I bent down slightly to get a better grip and the freezing water hit me higher up on my legs.

"Lift on three," David said. "One . . . two . . . three."

The television set came up and out of the water, dripping wet. It was as heavy as it looked, but I had so much adrenaline surging through my body I thought I could have lifted a car.

David backed toward the kitchen, pulling the television and me with him. The flashlight wobbled as we moved but didn't fall. The table was higher than the bottom of the television, and I strained to get my end high enough. We thumped it down. It now stood more than two feet above the water.

We both stood and stared at it for a few seconds.

"What do we do now?" David asked.

"I don't know," I said, shaking my head. I had no idea. "Do you want to try to save something else?"

"No, I mean, do we stay here or wake up Suzie and try to get out?"

"Out? Out there?" I said, gesturing toward the window.

"Yeah, maybe we should try to get up the valley."

"I don't know," I said. "Let's look outside."

I pulled out my flashlight and turned it back on. Carefully I moved toward the living room, following the beam of light reflecting off the water. My eye was caught again by more and more objects floating around in the house. I bent down and picked up Suzie's doll as it bobbed about in the water.

I tried to aim my flashlight through the front window, but the light just bounced back off the glass and I couldn't see anything.

"Let's open the door and look out," David said.

I felt a rush of panic—the door was protecting us—but then I realized that it was doing nothing. It wasn't holding back the water—the house was *full* of water. David struggled to open it.

We stepped onto the porch. David was just in his pyjamas and neither of us had a coat or shoes. The sky was still dark and ominous, but the rain had definitely slowed down. Despite everything, I was relieved. The worst was probably over. This was as deep as the water was going to get because hardly any more was falling.

We shone our lights out into the night. They managed to reach the houses on the other side of the street. What we could see in those narrow beams froze my soul. *All* of Raymore was under water, including the front lawns of all the houses we could see. The river had reached out and engulfed the whole street. There had to be three or four feet of water. We were in the middle of the river and we couldn't even see the shore. The water was surrounding the houses on the far side of the street, the side *away* from the river—or at least where the river was supposed to be.

From those houses I could see lights—flashlights and candles—flickers and pinpoints of light. I felt a little better. We weren't completely alone. I also heard voices. I couldn't make out words, but there were people calling out in the dark. Calling for help.

"There's a car on our lawn," David said. The words sounded so casual.

My beam spun to meet his. There was a dark-coloured sedan sitting on the corner of their lawn. The water was almost up to its windows.

A terrible thought raced through my mind: was it the McBrides' car? And if it was, where were they? Were they trapped inside? Had the storm taken them away? Or had they come home and gone to bed so quietly that I hadn't even heard them come in? Were they upstairs right now sleeping? I could go and wake them up and Mr. McBride would know what to do. I wouldn't have to be in charge, and—

"It's the Watsons' Chevy," David said. "From next door."

"But . . . why would they park it on *your* lawn?"

"Maybe they couldn't get it into their driveway or—it's moving!" David gasped.

Before our eyes the car started to shift. For a fleeting second I thought somebody was driving it, but then I realized that the car wasn't moving forward, or even backwards. It was moving *sideways*. It was being pushed down the street, down the river, and it had just come to a brief stop on their lawn before the current caught it again! It turned as it drifted, a slow circle. I kept my flashlight trained on it. The light caught the side mirror and bounced back to me eerily. It continued to spin slowly as it drifted, and then it simply disappeared from view, pushed along the street and around the corner.

"There's somebody in the water!" David screamed.

My head spun around faster than my flashlight and I followed his beam bouncing out over the water. There was something bobbing and weaving, racing along in the current, mostly hidden beneath the water. It was somebody caught in the current! No, it wasn't a person . . . at least not alive . . . there was something . . . somebody . . . it was a cow! The black-and-white markings were visible above the surface. It was a dead cow being pushed down the river, caught in the current, moving at a tremendous pace, being thrown about like a rag doll. It must have come from one of the farms north of Weston, caught and dragged downstream.

Our flashlights trapped other objects in the current: tree branches, pails and garbage cans, pieces of wood, things we couldn't make out, mostly submerged, and more dead animals. A little herd—three drowned sheep—raced down the middle of the street, being tossed and turned, head over hoof, as they passed.

"There's no way we could ever get across that current," I said, as much to myself as to David.

"We could if we had a boat."

"Do you have a boat?" I demanded.

"We have tools and some wood. We could hammer together some pieces to make something that could float, some kind of raft, and then we could paddle across."

"Look at the current. It's pushing around cars and cows. We couldn't fight against it, it would just catch us and take us down the river."

"But if we could just get to the other side of the street we'd be able to get out."

I looked at those houses opposite us. They weren't far away, but still they were on the other side of the current flowing down the middle of the street. Then I thought about the lights coming from those houses, and suddenly I understood.

"They can't get out either. Even if we could get over there we'd still be trapped," I said. "We have no choice. We have to stay here. This is our island."

"An island that's sinking."

"Not sinking. Flooding. We just have to head to higher ground. Come back inside."

It was bizarre to step into a house filled with water, but as David closed the door behind us I felt safer. We were in a flooded house, but it was still a house. *Safe as houses.*

We started up the stairs. I stopped. It wasn't just the first step—the first two were under water. Even though the rain had slowed down, the water was still rising. The butterflies in my stomach started fluttering again.

I counted the steps. There were twelve. Two below water and ten above. Ten steps that separated the top of our island from the flood water. My whole body was shaking. Was that from the cold or because I was scared? Probably both.

There was a loud crash and the whole house seemed to shake! I looked all around, playing the light in one direction and then another. I couldn't see anything. All I could think was that the kitchen table had collapsed and the television had smashed—splashed—onto the floor.

"What was that?" David asked.

I shook my head. "I thought it was the television falling."

"No, I don't think so. It was like something hit the side of the house."

He splashed off the step and through the water. Reluctantly, I stepped into the water once again and trailed behind David. He was trying to see out a little window at the side of the house.

"It's a truck," David said, his voice almost a whisper. "We've been hit by a truck."

What in the name of goodness was he talking about? I nudged him aside so that I could see. I gasped. There was a big panel truck pushed up against the side of the house. It had been carried down the river, and now the current was trapping it there.

David started giggling. I looked at him as if he were crazy, and then I realized that the whole thing *was* crazy. We were in a house filled with water, in the middle of a river that used to be a street, and the house had just been hit by a floating truck without a driver. I stiffened. It was abandoned . . . it didn't have a driver, did it?

I trained the beam of the flashlight onto the cab of the truck. At first the light was reflected back by the windshield and I couldn't see anything. I changed the angle slightly and then I could see inside. It was empty. Nobody in the driver's seat, nobody in the passenger's seat. I couldn't see the back of the vehicle, but there was nobody that I could see. And even if there had been somebody in there, dead or alive, what was I supposed to do? We were powerless to do anything except sit and watch.

That thought stuck in my mind. We weren't the only ones who were powerless. *Everybody* was powerless. Nobody could fight against this storm. Nobody could stop the force of the water. What was happening all around us was something that no person could stop, something that all the people of Weston, all the people of Toronto, all working together, couldn't stop. All we could do was wait it out, wait for the water to flow away, for the level to drop, for the current to slow, wait to be rescued. And until that happened, it was my job to keep David and Suzie safe.

"I'm going to check on Suzie."

"She's fine."

"I know, but I still want to check."

I also wanted to get out of the water, get to higher ground. Slowly I waded across the room and climbed the stairs. It felt good to get clear of the water again. I reached down and rubbed my legs.

They were so cold they were numb. I could hardly feel my feet at all. My shoes . . . where were my shoes? Were they under water behind the door or had they floated away? Did shoes float?

I jumped back into the water. I had to find my shoes. They were almost new and my mother had spent a lot of money on them and she'd kill me if anything happened to them. I bent down and felt around in the water behind the door. They weren't there.

I played the light around the room. There was so much floating around that it was hard to pick out—there! I spotted one of my shoes floating like a toy boat. I sloshed over and picked it up. Water drained out of it. I kept looking. One shoe wasn't much use without the other. There it was, in the corner, floating in a little fleet of household objects. I grabbed it. I'd found my shoes! My mother wouldn't be mad at me. Then I froze.

What would my mother be thinking right now? Was she asleep and unaware of what was happening to this house? Or was she standing up on the edge of the valley, looking down, terrified, worried to death about me? And what about the McBrides? Where were they? What were they thinking right now? I just wished I had some way of letting them all know that we were okay, that I was doing my job and taking care of the children.

My shoes and I mounted the stairs again. I stopped a few steps up and thought about putting them on, but decided I might as well carry them. Suzie's room was, of course, dark. I raised the flashlight just enough to see her without disturbing her. She was sound asleep, the covers pulled up tightly so that only her face was visible. Daisy, once again curled into a little ball at the foot of the bed, lifted her head slightly and looked at me. Her fur had dried, but the corner of the bedspread was damp. Her little nubby tail wagged happily. Both the dog and Susie were blissfully unaware. Ignorance is bliss. That was another thing my Nana used to say.

Satisfied that Suzie was safe, I decided that David should come upstairs too. I headed back down the steps, but stopped partway. David was still fishing things out of the water. For some reason my shoes had seemed important, but what he was doing seemed ridiculous.

"David, just leave it alone."

"I can't just stand here and do nothing. I have to try to do something."

I didn't want to go back into the water, but I knew I was going to. Even if I thought it was pointless, I couldn't let David work by himself. I was in charge and I had to help.

I took a few more steps down and then slipped and fell. I bumped down the last few steps and landed in the water! I jumped to my feet, completely soaked and freezing. In one hand I still held my flashlight. Despite the dip under water it was still working. But I'd dropped my shoes. They were floating away in front of me. I reached down and grabbed them again.

"What happened?" David sounded angry. He had probably been as startled and scared by my fall as I'd been.

"I must have missed a step or something."

I looked back at the stairs. They looked shorter . . . that didn't make any sense. I counted down from the top. There were only eight steps above the water. I looked down. The water was above my knees. It had suddenly gotten deeper, much deeper, almost a foot deeper.

I looked at David and then caught sight of movement in the front window. I did a double take. It was water, waves slapping against the glass, and as I watched in the beam of light I could see that the water was rising as I watched. It was like looking at an aquarium being filled up. David turned his flashlight onto the window too. As the water rose the glass seemed to be bulging inward. I stood there, frozen in place, icy water halfway up my thighs, mesmerized. And then the window shattered and exploded!

Before I could even think to react I was bowled over, knocked off my feet, and hurled across the room only to smash against the wall with a sickening thud. I tried to scream but the air in my lungs had been forced out, and as I opened my mouth water rushed in! I started to panic. I kicked my legs and tried to grab something to regain my balance but I couldn't fight the force of the water. There was a sudden pain in my back as I was bounced against something sharp, and then another searing shock as something else smashed into the side of my head. I felt like a sock in a washing machine, being bounced and battered, spun around, unable to right myself or gain control. My head was under water. My eyes were wide open but I couldn't see anything but black. I needed to get to the surface, I needed to get air, but I wasn't even sure which way was up.

My mind raced. This was it, right here, right now. I was going to die. I was going to drown. I stopped struggling, and almost immediately I popped to the surface.

I took a deep breath, filling my burning lungs. Desperately I looked around. All I could see clearly was the ceiling. It was just a foot or two above my head. The strong current swept me up and I thumped against the wall *above* the doorway leading into the kitchen. The water was pouring in through the front window and into the kitchen, and probably out the back window and back into the river. If I couldn't fight against it I'd be pulled out of the house. I had to get to higher ground, up the stairs.

I caught the faint outline of the chain from a light hanging down from the ceiling. If I could reach it I'd be that much closer to the stairs. I pushed off the wall and surged forward, grabbing the chain. I felt it give slightly but then it held, anchoring me in place. Now I had to move the rest of the way. I tried to orient myself. The stairs were just over to the left. I could try to fight the current, and if I failed and was swept backwards I'd still be able to grab the chain. I knew I had to move now while I still felt strong enough. I'd have to make one last push and just hope.

And then there was a light. And in that light I saw David. He was climbing up the stairs, a flashlight in his hand illuminating the route to safety. I let go of the chain and swam forward toward him. I dug in with my hands, clawing at the water and kicking with all my might until I thumped into the stairs. I started to pull myself up. A hand reached down and grabbed me and pulled me up. My knees knocked painfully against the steps until I tumbled forward, up the stairs, out of the water. I landed on top of David on the floor—the second floor.

"Th . . . thanks," I gasped.

He nodded his head but didn't answer. His mouth was wide open and he was panting. I could see his face. His eyes were open as wide as his mouth. He looked scared. No, he looked *terrified*.

"I . . . I . . . was trapped . . . I couldn't get out . . . I couldn't breathe," he said, his voice barely louder than a whisper.

"Me neither," I said as I struggled to sit up. "It just caught me . . . I thought I was going to get pushed out into the river. Your arm!"

David held up his right arm to examine a big gash below the elbow, using the beam of the flashlight. "I don't know . . . I don't know what happened . . ."

"Does it hurt?"

He shook his head. "I can't feel anything. It just feels numb . . . everything feels numb." He lowered his arm again and looked straight at me. "The water . . . it just exploded . . . it shot me across the room . . . into the wall . . . I hit the wall."

"Me too. It knocked the wind out of my lungs."

"But . . . what happened?"

I shook my head. "I don't know. I thought we were safe."

"Are we safe now?"

I peered down the stairs. It was like looking into a dark, watery cave. I couldn't see anything except the surface of the water a couple of steps from the top. Wait, how many steps were above the water when we crawled up?

I stared intently at the water. It bubbled and boiled as it bounced against the steps. It was hard to judge just how high it was and if it was rising or . . . wait, the second stair from the top was now completely under water. It was definitely still rising!

"Get Suzie up, now!" I screamed.

David jumped up and ran into Suzie's room. "Suzie, Suzie!" he yelled. I rushed in after him. She was sitting up in her bed, her eyes wide open, a look of fear and confusion on her face. I reached down and scooped her up, blankets and all. Daisy thumped down onto the floor.

Suzie started crying. I wanted to calm her, explain what was happening, but I couldn't do either. I didn't understand it myself, and I was fighting to stop *myself* from bursting into tears.

Suddenly I realized that there was water on the floor. In just a few seconds the water had climbed up the stairs and was gathering on the floor under our feet.

"We have to get higher!"

"The only thing higher than this is the roof," David said anxiously.

"Then we have to get up there."

"But how?" he demanded.

I went over to the window as quickly as I could. Between the water on the floor and Suzie in my arms I had to be careful not to fall. The water was boiling by, just below. I couldn't see anything. My flashlight was long gone, along with my shoes.

"I need light!" I shouted over my shoulder to David.

David rushed over and pointed his light out the window. There was an overhang from the roof. Even if there were some way of getting up the wall, there'd be no way of getting past that overhang.

"I don't think we can do it. I don't see any way."

"But we can't stay here. The water is still rising."

He was right. I could feel the water washing over my toes.

"Maybe we could go through the window and hang onto something that floats," David said. "Maybe we could take some wood or—"

"Look out there!" I screamed, nearly panicking now. "We wouldn't be able to hold on . . . we'd be washed away."

Suzie started wailing even more loudly.

"Maybe there's another way," David said.

"What? What other way?"

He pointed the beam of light up to the rafters. Between us and the roof were the finished beams, exposed because Mr. McBride had never finished the ceiling.

"Up there," he said. "We have to get up there."

I nodded my head in agreement.

I turned Suzie so that I could look straight into her face. Her eyes were tightly closed, as if she'd decided that anything she couldn't see happening around her wasn't real.

"Suzie," I said, trying to sound as calm as I could. "I need you to stop crying."

She pressed her face against my shoulder and kept on sobbing.

"Suzie, I need you to listen to me."

She started to cry even more loudly.

"Suzie, I have to put you down so that I can—"

She wrapped her arms and legs around me in a death grip.

"Suzie, please! I need you to—"

"No, don't put me down!" she screamed into my ear, and she tightened her grip around my neck, her fingers digging in.

"Suzie!" David yelled. "Smarten up and stop acting like a baby!"

"I'm not a baby!"

"Then stop acting like one, *now!*"

David grabbed her and her arms dropped away from me. He plopped her on the floor and her feet splashed down into the water. It was rising rapidly. I had to think, fast, and for all of us. I had to get them—and myself—out of this freezing water, somewhere dry, as high up as we could go.

I picked Suzie up again and put her on the desk in the corner. "Stay there, okay, Suzie?"

Turning to David I said, quietly, "We're going to climb up there into the rafters and get Suzie up there. Go get some dry clothes on—fast!"

I yanked open the top drawer of Suzie's dresser and pulled out three pairs of socks. I grabbed sweaters out of the middle drawer and took them to Suzie. "Get dressed up as warm as you can, Suzie—like you're going to go play in the snow. I'll be right back."

I sloshed back out and into the McBrides' bedroom. Thank heavens Mrs. McBride wasn't much bigger than me! I pulled a pair of plaid trousers off a hanger and struggled into them, dropping my soaking skirt into the water. Then I grabbed a cardigan and some socks from her dresser and ran back into Suzie's room. David was already sitting on the desk beside Suzie. Instead of his pyjamas he was wearing his jeans with a shirt and sweater and thick wool socks.

I handed the desk chair to him. "David, climb up onto this chair and get into the beams. I need you to help Suzie get up there."

He handed me the flashlight and I shone the beam on the chair. He stood up on the desk, and then climbed onto the chair. He reached up, grabbed one of the beams, and in one motion swung himself up. He took a seat on one of the rafters, his legs dangling over.

I started to climb onto the desk next to Suzie.

"What about Daisy?" Suzie sobbed.

Daisy! I'd forgotten all about the dog. I swung the light around the room and found Daisy back on Suzie's bed, all curled up in a ball. I aimed the flashlight right at her and her eyes glowed gold. She turned her head away from the light, like it was keeping her awake, and then laid it back down on the bed! That dog was trying to go to back to sleep!

We couldn't just leave Daisy there on the bed, but there was no way that she could balance in the rafters. Wait . . . I had an idea.

"Hold this," I said to Suzie, and I handed her the flashlight.

I dragged Suzie's little bed to the middle of the room. Daisy opened one eye, as if she were asking what I was doing.

"Move!" I screamed at the dog as I knocked her off the bed and onto the floor.

I grabbed the mattress off the bed and struggled to lift it up. It flopped and bent. It was heavier than I'd thought, but I had to lift it. Finally I dropped one end into the water on the floor, propped the rest on my back, and aimed it up to the rafters.

"Take this," I yelled to David. "Put it across the beams and we can use it for a perch to hold the dog."

I pushed the one end up and David steered it into the rafters. Even with both of us working it was heavy and awkward to move. He heaved it up and threaded it through one set of rafters and then guided it so it sat on three different beams.

"I don't know if this is going to work," David said. "It might not be strong enough to hold any weight."

"I don't see what else we could use." I tried to think. "Wait, yes I do!"

I ran out of the room. Leaning against the wall in the hallway was a piece of plywood. I grabbed it and dragged it back into the room.

"Put this over the beams!" I lifted it up. It was heavy but nowhere near as heavy or awkward as the mattress had been. David set it down on the beams. It formed a perfect little perch, a platform, a nest.

The water was now half a foot deep. We had to get Suzie up into the rafters. She was sitting on the desk, her arms wrapped around her knees, her face buried, rocking. She was still holding the flashlight but it was pointed aimlessly at the floor.

I moved in close, my mouth by her ear, and wrapped my arms around her. "It's okay, Suzie, we're going to be okay," I said softly. "We're going to go up there," I said, pointing at the beams. "It's like a little treehouse we made just for you and David and Daisy and me."

She looked up at the little platform.

"Maybe I can convince your parents that you and I can even sleep up there tomorrow night. Wouldn't that be fun?"

She didn't answer, but I detected a little smile.

"But tomorrow night it will just be you and me and Daisy. Just the girls. No boys allowed. And we'll sit up there, and if David comes into your room we'll throw things at him."

"Could we gob on him?" she asked.

"Of course. A great big green gob, right on his head!"

She started to laugh.

"But first we have to try it out. You go up first, then I'll help Daisy up, and then I'll come. Okay?"

I climbed up onto the desk. It felt good to have my feet out of the freezing water. My legs felt numb. My whole body felt numb.

"I'm going to lift you, and then David is going to help pull you up. Ready?"

She climbed up on the chair and then I lifted her into the air as high as I could reach. David grabbed both of his sister's hands and pulled. She sailed up and away and he put her down on the platform.

"Well, do you like your nest?" I called up.

She nodded. "Daisy."

"Sure. I'll pass her up."

I turned around. I had expected her to be sitting on the bed again, but she was gone! I played the flashlight all around the room. The water was rising and there were now toys floating about, but there was no Daisy. Where had that stupid dog gone? I jumped back down into the cold water and sloshed into the hall. Water was rushing, boiling, up the stairwell. I waded down the hall, flashing the light into David's room.

"Daisy!" I yelled. I expected her to be on his bed, but there was nothing there but the crumpled up sheets.

"She's over here!" David yelled out.

"Where?" I called back.

"Here, in my mom and dad's room!" David was standing on the beams above his parents' bedroom.

I rushed in. Daisy was curled up on Mr. and Mrs. McBride's bed. I grabbed her by the collar and dragged her off her feet. She strained against me as I pulled her off the bed, struggling to try to climb back up, but I held tightly onto her collar and towed her along through the water. Daisy fought me all the way, angry that she had to wade through the water. She even snarled at me, and I was so surprised I almost let go. She snarled again and started growling. Using my free hand I splashed water into the dog's face.

"Daisy!" Suzie called out. "Good girl!"

Yeah, good dog. Stupid dog.

I grabbed her around her tubby middle and plopped her down on the desk and then I climbed up beside her, keeping one hand on her collar to stop her from running off again. Actually, there was probably no chance of her jumping down into the water.

"I'll pass her up."

I stood up on the desk and again gathered the dog in my arms and heaved her. She was heavy. A few more walks and a few less snacks would have been a good thing. David reached down and grabbed her. Then he pulled her up and placed her on the mattress.

Carefully I climbed onto the chair. I reached up and grabbed one of the rafters. I started to pull myself up but my arms began to quiver and I felt my energy start to fade. I didn't have the strength to pull myself up . . . my arms felt so weak . . .

"Here," David called out. He grabbed me by the back of the sweater, tugging it partially over my head as he pulled. I fell onto the platform between him and Suzie.

"Thanks," I gasped. "I feel weak . . . tired."

"The cold water sucks away all your energy," David said. "That's what kills people when they fall into cold water. They get so weak they can't swim any more and they drown. How cold do you think the water is?"

"Not freezing, but really cold. How's your arm?"

"It doesn't hurt. My whole arm is numb. It doesn't feel like anything. It's like it isn't even my arm." He turned his arm over so we could both see it better. There was a six-inch-long gash on his right forearm. I couldn't tell how deep the cut was but I could see that it was still dripping blood down his arm, onto his jeans and onto the platform.

"I just wish we could clean it up, maybe tape some gauze on it."

"We have all that stuff in our first-aid kid . . . if you can get it."

The last thing in the world I wanted to do was go back down there, but if I had to, I had to. "Where is it?"

"First you go to the stairs," he said. "Then take a really big breath, jump in, and swim to the kitchen.

I think it's in the drawer two over from the sink on the right side."

"You're joking."

"No, I'm pretty sure that's the right drawer. And since you're in the kitchen anyway, you might as well get me a soda, too."

I opened my mouth in disbelief. He couldn't really think that I should—

"Elizabeth, I'm kidding. I don't even want a soda."

"I do," Suzie said. "Can I have one too? I'm thirsty."

"No sodas, Suzie. Will you settle for a drink of water?" David asked. "We have plenty of that."

"I don't want water."

"Nobody on Raymore Drive wants water, but a soda is a little bit out of reach right now."

This was crazy. Why was he joking around? Didn't he know how serious this was? The worse things got, the more he seemed to be joking around.

Then I thought about how that was the way he always acted—with me, with kids at school, with his teacher. Always joking, always saying things that got him in trouble. Maybe that wasn't him trying to show what a cool kid he was—maybe he was acting that way because he was scared. He'd left behind his old neighbourhood, his school, and all his friends to come here to a whole new world. I would have been scared if I'd been him.

I was scared *now*. David was too. He didn't show it, but he had to be. But maybe he was doing the right thing. His acting like it was a joke helped to keep me calm, to keep Suzie calm.

I looked down. The floor was about eight feet down. There was maybe two feet of water on the floor. We had six feet of safety. Above us, the roof was another three or even four feet up, more at the very peak. That meant we had ten or twelve feet of air. Would that be enough, or would the water rise so high that we'd be pushed right up, trapped, drowned? I couldn't imagine the water rising that much more . . . but a few hours ago I couldn't have imagined *any* of this ever happening.

How much had the water already risen now? Fifteen feet, twenty feet? All I knew was that it had flooded all the way from the river, up to the height of the backyard, up over the porch, all the way up the stairs to the second floor. If it had come that far, maybe it could come farther, rise higher. What would we do? We needed some way out.

"I'll be back," I said as I started to slide off the mattress.

"Where are you going?" David grabbed me by the arm.

"I'm going to get a soda. You sure you don't want one?"

"Seriously, where are you going?"

"I'm just going down for a minute."

He let go of my arm. I grabbed one of the beams and carefully lowered myself onto the chair on top of the desk. David lit my way with the flashlight.

I sloshed down to the floor. The water sent shivers up my legs and into my spine.

All around my feet, floating in the water, were Suzie's toys and clothes, and some pieces of wood. I was looking for a specific piece. I took one that was heavy but just a little more than two feet long. I held it firmly and waded over to the window. I smashed the wood against the glass and it shattered!

"What are you doing?" David demanded.

The whole bottom pane of glass was smashed out, leaving behind broken and jagged pieces hanging from the frame.

"Why are you doing that?" David yelled again.

"I thought we could use some fresh air." He wasn't the only one who could joke around.

Next I knocked out the jagged pieces, opening up the entire frame. It was a clean, big hole, big enough that I could fit my whole body through it if I needed to. Now if the water kept rising we'd at least have a way out. We wouldn't be trapped up there in the rafters, pushed up, suffocated, drowned. Now, if we had to, we could get through that window. Through the window and into the river. Out of the frying pan and into the fire. That was another thing my Nana always said.

I lay on my back with my eyes closed. It really didn't matter whether they were open or closed because I couldn't see anything in the pitch-black. The flashlight had been dimming and we needed to save the batteries, so we were keeping it off except for periodic checks of the water level. What would we have done without it? I wished I'd been able to keep hold of mine, but figured I was lucky to get out with my life.

Being in the dark should have made it seem scarier, but strangely it seemed safer. I could pretend that this wasn't happening. Instead, I could imagine that we were tucked away in a little cave, far away from danger. I guess in some ways there was a cave-like quality to where we were. We were in a pocket of air, a little dry spot suspended above the water . . . so . . . more like a nest. That was what I'd told Suzie to think of it as—a nest, or a treehouse. I'd just pretend that we were three little birds in our nest, and soon we'd be able to take to the air and fly away.

Suzie was pressed tightly against me on one side. She hadn't moved for a while and I decided that she'd drifted back to sleep. I would have enjoyed that escape. Daisy was lying partially beside and partially on top of me. I didn't mind. The warmth of her body felt good. I knew David was just a few inches away on the other side of Suzie. I could sense his presence, and that felt good as well. Occasionally he'd move, trying to get more comfortable or warmer, and the movement would radiate throughout the little platform.

At least my feet felt warm with two pairs of Mrs. McBride's socks on.

I pressed my eyes closed even tighter. I could close off the sights, but there were still the sounds. I could hear the rushing of the river around us in all directions. It was as though we were standing on the footbridge again. That sound was everywhere and constant, and it just kept getting louder and louder as the water rose higher and higher.

Worse than the sound of the river were the unpredictable crashes and smashes as objects struck the house. The first few times that it happened I startled and jumped slightly. That wasn't a good way to react, especially for Suzie's sake. David just kept making jokes about how maybe all the neighbours were parking their cars on his lawn. Jokes and more jokes.

There was another crash as something slammed against the side of the house. This time I hardly reacted. How bizarre. Those sounds, those things, could have been cars, or trucks, or tree branches, or whole trees, or anything and everything in the whole valley. Short of a house, what was there that the river couldn't pick up and carry away?

"I'm going to turn the flashlight on again," David said.

The little flashlight wasn't much, but after the pitch-blackness it seemed incredibly bright.

David rolled over and focused the beam on the water below.

"How is it?" I asked, hoping to hear that it was lower or at least the same, but afraid to hear his answer.

"Not good. Look."

I didn't want to look. I wanted to tightly close my eyes.

"It's deeper."

"Are you sure?" I asked.

"Look for yourself."

I opened my eyes and rolled over so I could look too. He had the beam aimed at the window. Of course he was right. The water was now flowing in through the broken-out pane. I felt sick. There was still room before the water reached the top but less than a foot before the whole window would be submerged, and the only way out and up to the surface would be to dive down and into the muddy, freezing water. We'd be under water, fighting our way to a raging, flooding river, a river that was ripping out trees and tossing cars around like they were toys. And what would happen to us when we got out? What chance would *we* have in a current that strong?

I looked over at Suzie. Sleeping, she looked like a little angel. She *was* a little angel. What chance would she have? She could never survive the current. How terrible would it be for me to somehow survive and for Suzie to drown? How would I tell her parents, what words would I say, how could I ever face them? How could I live with all that guilt? Then again, I really didn't have to worry about any of that. It wasn't like *I* was going to survive, either.

That thought reverberated in my brain. I was going to die. We were all going to die.

Sure, I knew in my head that I was going to die *someday*. Everybody died. I'd just thought it was going to be a million years from now when I was old—maybe in my sixties or my seventies, like my Nana, who'd lived to be seventy-seven. I'd never thought that it would happen when I was thirteen. Tonight. Maybe in a few hours.

All at once I felt tears come to my eyes. I turned away and tried to hide them but I couldn't hold back a big sob.

"Are you crying?" David asked.

"No," I answered, trying to sniffle the tears back.

"There's nothing to cry about," he said.

"I'm *not* crying."

He chuckled. "Sure you're not, and it isn't raining, either. But it would be okay if you did . . . I'd understand."

"You would?"

"I know how bad it is. I'm not an idiot . . . I'm scared too."

I almost instinctively blurted out that I wasn't scared, but that would have been stupid. As stupid as denying that I had been crying.

"We just don't have time for tears. We need to figure out what to do," he said.

"There's nothing we *can* do except wait, and hope, and pray."

"You do that, and I'll try to figure a way out. I think our best chance is if we hang onto something that floats," David said.

"What?" I asked, hearing the words but not understanding what he meant.

"Our best chance to survive out on the river is if we can hang onto something that floats," he repeated.

"You thinking about building a boat again?"

"More like a raft. We have enough wood."

He was right. Floating throughout the whole upstairs were pieces of wood that were going to be used to finish the walls and ceiling.

"We have the wood, but how would you join the pieces together?" I asked.

"We have lots of nails and tools up here." He paused. "Well . . . down there on the floor, under the water."

"A lot of good that'll do us."

"I *could* get them."

I couldn't imagine going down there into the water. A chill ran up my spine just thinking about it. And I couldn't let him go down there, either.

"Even if you could build something, you wouldn't be able to get it through the window. How would you get it outside?"

"I hadn't thought about that. I guess I could still tie a couple of boards together. That would be better than nothing."

"But I don't think you could attach enough to keep any of us afloat. It was a good idea, though," I offered.

"If only we'd gotten out sooner. We could have just waded out when the water was only a foot or so deep. We would have been safe."

"We didn't know what was going to happen," I said. "And by the time we did, it was too late to try to leave. You saw what Raymore was like. There was no way we could have crossed that current."

"We should have known better, and we should have left sooner, that's all I'm saying."

He was right—and it was my fault. I was the one in charge and I should have known.

"But I'm not blaming you," he said, as if he'd been reading my thoughts. "Nobody knew. Not your parents. Not my parents. Nobody. Don't you think the police or fire department would have gone from house to house and made us leave if they'd thought this might happen?"

"I guess so," I said, feeling a little better.

"I just feel bad, you know, about Suzie being here. I just wish she were someplace else, safe." He paused. "I'm going to turn out the light again."

"Probably wise."

The dark overwhelmed us. Every time he turned off the flashlight the darkness seemed thicker and heavier. I felt my heart race, and despite the chill in the air I felt my whole body flush. I knew it would take a minute or so for my eyes to become accustomed to the dark before I could start to see shadows and shades again, but until that happened I felt vulnerable and unsure.

"I'm hungry," David said.

"I think there's some meatloaf left if you want to go down to the kitchen," I said, trying to joke around a bit myself.

"I didn't like it when my mother made it in the first place, and it didn't taste any better today."

Lying there in the dark, it was at least reassuring to hear another voice.

"What time do you think it is?" I asked.

"I don't know. It could be midnight or it could be later. You got someplace you're supposed to be?"

"Just trying to figure out how long before it gets light."

"Could be five or six hours or more. What time does the sun come up?"

"Just before seven . . . I think."

"And you figure if we can last until morning then we'll be okay, right?" he asked.

"I guess so. They'll be able to send boats out to rescue people."

"Boats work in the dark," David said, "if they knew we were here to rescue . . . but nobody knows."

"Our parents know."

"I'd hate to be them," he said.

"Why? You don't think they're in any danger, do you?"

David laughed. "I figure that no matter where they are, they have to be in less danger than us. They're probably up on the hill, watching, going crazy worried about us. We know we're okay, but they don't know anything."

David was right. *We* knew we were still alive, but what must they be thinking? If they were up on the hill they'd know just how bad things were, that the house had practically disappeared beneath the water, but they wouldn't know anything about us.

Thank goodness they were safe . . . my parents had to be safe. There was no way that the river had risen high enough to even touch our house. My father had said that the McBrides' television antenna wouldn't get good reception because it wasn't as high as the edge of the valley, and our house was above that level. My parents were certainly safe.

I just hoped my father wasn't trying something crazy. He wasn't good at waiting, and I couldn't imagine him just standing up there on the hill, doing nothing. I just had to hope that my mother would convince him to stick it out. At least we didn't own a boat or he might have been trying to put it into the river. No boat could survive that current in the dark. It would be crazy to even try.

I pictured them sitting around the kitchen table, listening to the radio, waiting for things to change. This would all end and then I'd get home. I'd get out of these wet and filthy clothes, and after I'd finished the snack my mother made I'd take a really long, hot bubble bath. A bath. I wanted to get away from all this by lying in a big puddle of water? I started to chuckle.

"What's so funny?" David asked.

"I was just thinking how good a bath would be."

"If you don't mind it being cold it can be arranged."

"I was hoping for hot, with bubbles."

"The bubble part could have happened too if you'd fed us beans for supper instead of leftover meatloaf."

"I'll try to remember that for the next time."

"Do you know what's even stranger?" David asked.

"What?"

"I really, really have to pee."

I started laughing again.

"This isn't funny."

"I think it's pretty funny, but if you have to go, you have to go."

"Here?"

"Can't think of anyplace else. Go over the edge."

"With you sitting here?"

"Do you expect me to leave the room? It's pitch-black. I can't even see you."

He didn't answer but I felt his weight shift slightly.

"Be careful," I warned.

"I've been doing this for a long time so I think I've pretty well got it mastered."

"Have you ever done in it the dark while leaning out of the rafters over a flooded bedroom?"

"Okay, okay. I'll be careful."

I heard the soft sound of a zipper, then a few seconds later the sound of a steady stream of water hitting water below. It went on, and on, and on, pausing for a half second and then resuming again. David was taking one truly amazing pee. Finally it stopped for good.

"We'd better check to see if you caused the water level to rise," I said.

"I told you I really had to go. But seriously, we should check the level anyway."

David clicked on the flashlight again. Now he was lying on his belly, looking down.

"Well?"

"Still rising."

"How much higher?"

"A few more inches."

"A few inches that fast?" I asked.

"Yeah, but listen."

I turned my head slightly to one side. What did he want me to listen for? "I just hear the river."

"Exactly. I can hardly hear the rain any more."

He was right. I could still hear the rain hitting against the roof, but it wasn't nearly so loud.

"If it's almost stopped raining, shouldn't the water level stop rising and start to go down?" he asked.

"I guess all the water that's fallen everywhere is still running downhill to get to the river. It still hasn't arrived yet."

"I hadn't thought about that. That means that even if it stops raining completely the water level could still keep rising. Right?"

I knew that was right, but I almost didn't want to admit it. "Yeah. We could have the water rising for hours to come."

"And do you think it could rise this much?" he asked, gesturing first to the water below and then to the ceiling above our heads.

I shook my head. "I wish I knew."

"I really didn't expect you to know. I think the only real question is, should we try to get out?"

"Not yet. The river might not rise much more."

"Do you believe that?"

"I just know we should stay here as long as possible. We're better off in here than out there."

"The longer we wait, the harder it's going to be to get out if we do have to leave. Are you a good swimmer?"

"Pretty good. You?"

"I can hold my own. I'm just worried about Suzie. She doesn't even like getting her face in the water."

"Sounds like Daisy . . . what about Daisy?" I asked. "Can dogs dive?"

"I've been thinking about that. Maybe if I have her on the leash I can drag her down and through the window."

"Do you really think that would work?"

"I don't know, but I can't just leave her here to drown without trying something."

We were both silent for a moment.

"Well?" David asked. "So what do we do?"

I wanted to stay right where we were. The last thing in the world I wanted to do was dive into that cold, dark water and hope I could surface in the middle of the river. Last thing in the world . . . and if I made the wrong decision, it *would* be the last thing I'd ever do, the last thing that any of us would ever do. My decision would determine not just if I would live, but David, and Suzie, and even Daisy, too.

Then I realized that there might not be a right answer. No matter what I decided, we still might die. It wasn't that one way was necessarily right and the other wrong. It could be that both were wrong, that there was *no* way out of this. I felt a rising sense of panic. What if there was no right answer, and no matter what I decided we were dead anyway? It felt as if the air in our little pocket was getting thinner. I was struggling to draw a full breath. I tried to slow down my breathing, slow down my beating heart.

"Do we stay or do we go?" David asked.

"We stay," I croaked. "For now, we stay."

"I hope you're right."

"Do *you* think we should go?" I asked, suddenly doubting my decision.

"No, I think you're right."

"Good. Maybe you should turn out the flashlight again."

The light disappeared and we were submerged in black once more.

"You ever think about dying?" David asked after a few minutes.

"We're not going to die," I replied, trying to sound as calm and confident as possible.

"I don't mean now, I mean ever. Do you ever think about dying?"

"Sometimes, I guess, but not very often."

"I didn't used to think about it. At least not before we moved here."

"Moving to Weston made you think about dying?"

"Not moving to Weston. Moving away from Toronto. It felt like my life was over."

"Was it that hard?"

"Have you ever had to move?" he asked.

"I've lived in my house my whole life."

"I'd lived in our house for my whole life. That was my home. That's where I knew all the neighbours, and the school, and my classmates, my friends. Coming up here, it was like I had died."

"That's rough."

"It was more than rough." He paused. "So, do you want to be buried or burned? What do they call it when you get burned?"

"Cremation."

"Yeah, cremation. You want to be buried or cremated? I think cremation would be better."

"How come?"

"Sounds better than having your body eaten by worms, don't you think?"

I groaned as I pictured it.

"And then they could take the ashes and spread them wherever you wanted. Do you know where I'd want mine scattered?"

"In your old neighbourhood?"

"Yeah!" he exclaimed. "How did you know that?"

"I'm a genius, didn't I tell you?"

"Seriously, though, does that sound crazy?"

"Not really."

"So, do you want to be buried or burned?" David asked again.

"Neither."

"The only other choice I can see is if they stuff you. Maybe they could just do your head and your parents could mount it on the wall over the fireplace, like a moose or a deer."

That made me laugh. "I don't think that will work."

"That just leaves you with the two choices. Buried or cremated?"

"I really don't want to think about it."

"I think this is a really good time to think about it. Right now."

"It just seems a little morbid."

"Is it morbid for a ninety-nine-year-old man to be thinking about dying?" he asked.

"Of course not."

"Well, right now, right here, we might be closer to having to come up with an answer than the old man. It could be just hours away. We could die."

"*We're not going to die.*" It was Suzie's voice, startling me. The only reason we'd been talking about any of this was because she was asleep—or at least I'd thought she was asleep. How long had she been awake? How much of what we'd been talking about had she heard?

"Turn on the light," I said to David, and he instantly responded.

Suzie put a hand up to shield her eyes from the light. She looked so small.

"You're right, we *aren't* going to die," I said.

"I know that. Do you know why we're not going to die?" Suzie asked.

"Why?" David questioned.

"Because we have Elizabeth, and she's going to make sure we're okay. Right, Elizabeth?"

For a split second I hesitated. "That's right, nobody is allowed to die. I'm here to take care of you, and so is your brother. Do you think David would let anything hurt his little sister?"

"He's the one who usually *does* hurt me," she said.

"But I've seen him be nice to you sometimes," I said. "He plays with you and spends time with you."

"He mainly only spends time with me when he hits me more than once."

"I'm a big brother. That's my job," David joked.

I started to laugh again. There was something so normal, so reassuring about hearing the two of them bickering like there was nothing wrong, like there was no need for us to consider going down into the water and out to the river . . . wait . . . maybe there was another way of thinking about this.

"Hey, David, you know when you wash dishes?"

"I don't wash dishes. That's women's work."

I decided to ignore that remark—I needed to explain what I was thinking more than I needed to get into a fight.

"Anyway, if you take a glass, turn it upside down, and dip it into the water, do you know what happens?"

"It gets clean?"

"No, there's a pocket of air trapped in the glass. And because it has no place to go, it can't get out of the glass, and so the water can't get in. Maybe this is the same. The water has risen above the level of the windows so now the air is trapped in here and can't get out. Even if the water rises above the roof we'll be right here in this pocket of air!" I felt a rush of relief. We were safe! We could stay in our little nest and never have to swim out into the river!

"What would happen if the glass had a hole in the bottom where the air could get out?" David asked.

"Well . . . then the water would get in. It wouldn't work," I said.

"Then it isn't going to work here, either. The roof has holes in it."

"But it's a roof, it stops the rain . . . doesn't it?"

"It did until my father put up the television antenna. He made holes to attach it and to run the wire down into the house, and now the roof leaks because he didn't patch the holes the right way."

My heart sank. "Too bad the holes aren't big enough for us to get through."

We were quiet again. "Hold on," David said. "Maybe there *is* a way that we can get through one of those holes."

David suddenly stood up. He had to hunch his back to avoid hitting his head against the roof. He stepped off the platform and onto one of the beams, holding the flashlight in one hand and placing the other against the roof for balance. He took another step, stretching out to reach the next rafter.

"What are you doing?" I asked, as I carefully stood up too.

"Thought I'd go for a walk. You should join me."

"I think I'll stay right here, thank you."

"Actually, that wasn't just an invitation. I really need you to come along too. I can't do it without you."

He had made his way over until he was standing over top of the bathroom. He was moving effortlessly, quickly, and stopped when he reached his parents' bedroom.

"I'm not going anywhere until you tell me what you're doing."

He tapped the roof. "We're getting out this way."

I rapped it with my own knuckles. "Wood. How are we going to get through solid wood?"

"That's why I'm over here."

"Is there a way out over there?" I asked hopefully, although the question itself made no sense.

The roof might have been leaky, but of course there was no way there was a hole big enough for us to fit through.

He pointed the flashlight down into the water. "Matter of fact, I think it's right about here. Come on, I need your help."

I reached up to the roof, using it for support and balance, and stretched my foot out over the gap between the beams until it was securely resting on the next one.

"Be careful, Elizabeth," Suzie warned me.

"I'll try." I drew over my other leg so I was standing, balanced on the beam. It wasn't very wide—only two or three inches—but it was wide enough to stand on. Slowly, carefully, I repeated the action to move to the next support.

"You planning on getting here anytime soon?" David asked.

"I'm just trying to avoid falling in."

Step by step, gap by gap, beam by beam I moved. Each time I looked down to make sure my footing was right and then moved my eyes upward. Looking down wasn't good. It wasn't the height as much as the water. It was moving, swirling, dark, and impenetrable. This was much worse than crossing the footbridge. In the light from David's flashlight I could make out the images of objects beneath the surface; the toilet and bathtub gleamed an eerie white, but I couldn't see the floor beneath them.

Finally I stood beside David. "What now?"

"I need you to hold the flashlight for me. Aim it straight down, right there."

I took the flashlight. "What good will that do? It's just water."

"It's what's below the water. We're standing right overtop of my father's tool chest."

I looked harder, following the light down and then into the water. It only penetrated a foot or two at best. Below that was darkness.

"I don't see it," I said.

"Me neither, but I'm pretty sure it's right down there."

"So close, but so far."

"Not so close, but not so far."

He ducked down, and for a split second I thought he was going to fall. I reached out to grab him—and missed. But he was sitting down on the beam. His feet were hanging down, swinging, just above the water . . . just barely above. That meant that the water had risen even more and was still rising fast, maybe even faster. I looked for a reference point. I couldn't see the windows in his parents' bedroom at all because they were well below the waterline.

"Hold the light straight down."

"Sure, but why?"

"I'm going to need help to find my way back."

"Back from—"

Before I could finish my sentence he'd swung down and splashed into the water! He was holding onto the beam with his hands, but his lower body was in the water.

"What are you, crazy?" I screamed.

"I'm going to go and get some tools. It's the only way."

"But you can't! What about the current? You might be swept out through one of the windows!"

"There's hardly any current now. Look, see how things are just floating, hardly moving?"

The whole surface of the water was covered with debris. Toys and clothes, things that had floated up from the kitchen, pieces of wood. They were just bobbing on the surface. David was right. There wasn't any current . . . at least at the top.

"I can do it," David said. "Just hold the light steady . . . please." His voice quavered over the last word. I knew his bravery was an act. He was scared and cold, but he was determined to do what he thought needed to be done.

Hand over hand he moved across the beam, and I started to move the light along with him.

"No, don't do that!" he said firmly. "The light has to shine straight down, okay?"

I didn't answer. I just trained the light back where he wanted it.

He kept moving over toward the wall. "I'm pretty sure that I'm standing on top of my parents' tall dresser. This is how I'm going to get into the water and back out." He took one hand off the rafter and swung down as low as he could reach, rocking slightly, and—

"There it is! I can feel it with my toe!"

He let go of the beam. He teetered back and forth but then came to a stop, his back against the wall. He was standing in chest-deep water, but he was still standing, his head and shoulders just above the water.

"Keep the flashlight exactly where it is."

He raised his hands above his head as though he was going to dive in, and then he hesitated for a second, and another and another. I could only imagine what was going through his mind. If it had been me, it would have been total panic and fear. Then, with a big splash, he dove in and disappeared into the murky water! I'd known it was coming, but I was so startled that I almost screamed out. I kept my hand firm and the light aimed straight down. It was the only thing I could do to help.

"David?" Suzie called out. She sounded as scared as I felt. "David!" she wailed.

"He can't hear you. He's under the—"

He broke the surface with a splash right under the beam of light, pushing aside a piece of wood that had drifted overtop. He looked as if he were caught in a spotlight.

"He's up! He's okay!" I yelled to Suzie.

"It's down there, right underneath my feet," he said.

He took a deep breath and dove down again, and his feet were the last things that I saw before he disappeared under the water. He was gone. I couldn't see him or any sign of him. I stared down at the surface of the water and started to count silently. One . . . two . . . three . . . four . . . five . . . six . . .

He came to the surface again, shooting out of the water before settling in to tread water.

"I got it open!" he said excitedly. "I got the chest open! Now I've just got to get out some tools. I need a hammer, or even better a hatchet or an axe."

"Are all of those in the tool chest?"

"There'll be a hammer for sure, and I know my dad owns a hatchet and an axe. I think the axe was in the shed by the woodpile . . . where the woodpile was . . . but the hatchet might be in the tool chest. I'm going to go down and get it."

He took another deep breath and then dove back down.

"He's diving again," I called out to Suzie. "Your brother is a very good swimmer. He's getting the tools so we can cut through the roof. Isn't that good?"

"That's good," she replied.

I had been talking to distract and comfort Suzie, but it was doing the same for me. It made me feel better. I held the light firmly . . . he'd been down there a long time . . . longer than before.

He burst out of the water. "I got it!" he shrieked, his voice so loud that it echoed off the roof. In his hand was a hatchet—a little axe—and as he raised his hand above the water to show me, treading water, the weight pushed the rest of him down.

"How are you going to get back up?"

"Same way I got down . . . hold on." His hand and the hatchet dropped below the water. "There, I tucked it into my belt."

He swam over to the spot where he'd dropped down. He stopped swimming and was now, I assumed, standing on the dresser again.

"It's deeper," he said.

"It's always deeper."

"No, a lot deeper. Look."

Only his head was above water. A few minutes ago it had been his head and shoulders. The water was rising really fast, faster than before. I tried to do a quick calculation in my mind. If it had risen almost a foot in just a couple of minutes, how many minutes would it take to get up to the rafters, and then right up to the roof? I tried to spin the numbers around but I couldn't do it. All I knew was that we had to move fast. I wanted to yell to David, tell him how fast things were moving, but I couldn't do that. I couldn't warn him without scaring Suzie.

"Let me give you a hand," I said.

David jumped up and grabbed the beam, but his grip failed and he let go, landing back in the water, on the dresser.

"You have to jump higher!" I told him.

He jumped again. This time he got both hands on the beam and started to pull himself up, but again fell back, and his whole body disappeared into the murky water. He resurfaced again and paddled over to the spot above the dresser.

"Wait, I'll help." I had to help pull him up, but I needed both hands to do that. I couldn't hold the flashlight at the same time.

"Suzie, I need you to do something. I need you to hold the flashlight."

"Should I come there?"

"No!" I practically screamed. "I mean, no, thank you. I'll bring it to you. I just need you to aim it over this way as best as you can."

Carefully I started toward her. It was harder this time because I had only the one hand; the other was holding tightly to the flashlight. I wanted to make sure I didn't fall. Not just because I didn't want to go down into the water, but because I didn't want the flashlight to fall in. I could stand a dunk in the water, but I didn't know if the flashlight would survive being submerged again.

"Hurry," David called out. "It's really cold . . . really cold."

I only had two more rafters to negotiate. I stepped and then stepped again without stopping, so that I practically fell onto the mattress beside Suzie. Daisy jumped out of the way and almost toppled off the edge.

"Take it and aim it across so I can follow," I ordered Suzie.

I handed her the flashlight, but kept one hand on it. "Suzie, this is really important. Hold onto it with both hands. Whatever you do, you can't drop this. Understand?"

She nodded.

I started back through the rafters. Having both hands free made it much faster. I stopped when I was directly overtop of David. He was standing, tucked against the wall, and not much light was bouncing down. He looked up at me. He looked cold and scared. Carefully I lowered myself until I was sitting with my bottom on one beam and my feet on a second, perched there.

"Okay, now jump and this time I'll grab on and try to pull you up."

David reached out of the water. He jumped and grabbed the beam with both hands. I reached down and latched on to his arms. I struggled, holding tight and leaning backwards to use my weight to pull him up. He seemed to be hovering in mid-air, holding on, not gaining or losing ground, and then he surged upward. The sudden shift sent me sailing backwards and I had to lock my feet under the beam to stop myself from tumbling over as he heaved himself up beside me.

"You okay?" I asked.

"I'm okay . . . now," he gasped. His voice was shaky and his body was cold and he was shivering. "We gotta start chopping."

"You have to wait a minute, regain your strength."

"No time. We have to do it now . . . the water is almost to the rafters. We have to cut a hole before it's too late."

"Where do we chop?" I asked.

He looked around at the roof, first one way and then the other. "Over there," he said, pointing to a spot near the peak. "That's where the antenna is."

I could just see a black wire hanging down from the roof.

"The antenna will give us something to hang on to when we're on the roof. It's going to be pretty slick. It's also one of the highest spots. I think we're going to need that extra couple of feet before this is over."

David's teeth were chattering and he was shaking badly. He got to his feet but wobbled ever so slightly, and for a split second I though he was going to tumble over. I reached over and grabbed his leg to steady him.

"David, are you okay?"

"I'm fine . . . good . . . just cold. I thought it would be better when I got out of the water . . . but I'm still so cold."

"Maybe you should rest—"

"No time."

He started over to the spot where he wanted to chop. It was close to the peak of the roof and he was able to stand straight up. It would have been easier if he hadn't had to strike so high above his head, but he was right, the higher up the better.

He pulled the hatchet out of his belt loop, reached up, and smashed it against the roof. There was a tremendous noise that echoed around the small space. Then he did it again, and again.

"Is it working?" I asked.

"It isn't very sharp. It's just making little dents. Some light would help . . . but it would be better if I had a place to stand."

"Like a platform?"

"Yeah, exactly."

Floating in the water below were pieces of two-by-four. If we put a few of them together on top of the beams they'd make a perfect platform. I had to get them. I spun myself around, and then slowly lowered myself so that my feet were on one beam and my chest was on a second. I angled myself down, still wedging my body between them, holding on with one hand and reaching down with the other.

With each whack of the hatchet I could feel the whole structure shake, and the vibration went through the beams and into my body, nudging me forward. I kept having to wiggle my body back so I wouldn't fall head first into the water. Precariously balanced and leaning forward the way I was, it felt even more dangerous.

I was just able to reach down to the water. If only it were a little bit higher. How bizarre, wanting the river to rise higher! I grabbed the edge of a two-by-four and pushed it forward just a shade. I dared to lean a little bit farther and secured my grip. I started to fish it out, leaning backwards as I pulled it out of the water to counterbalance the weight. It was a big piece, over six feet long, and I had to angle it up and then over the one beam, laying it down on two so it made a narrow platform. I grabbed a second piece, and then a third and a fourth, placing each one beside the others on the two beams. I should have been getting more tired with the strain of pulling them up but the success seemed to give me energy.

I rose to my knees and then shifted the boards forward one by one until finally I had moved them all to just beside David. He was balanced, one foot on one beam and the second on another, still chopping, although the pace of his blows had slowed down considerably.

"Take a break," I said.

He didn't argue. He bent over, breathing heavily.

"Watch out." I pushed the boards over, one by one, until the platform was right underneath where he'd been working.

"That should make it easier," he said. "I'll start again in a few seconds . . . my body is still freezing but my arms are burning."

"You've been working hard."

"I'm not making much progress."

The boards right above David were splintered and dented but he hadn't been able to forge even a small hole.

"Let me take over for a while," I offered.

He handed me the hatchet and I got to my feet. The boards sagged as I stood.

"Can I come over?" Suzie called out.

"Maybe you'd better stay with Daisy," David replied.

"Daisy could come over too."

"Not unless she can fly."

"You could help move the platform the way Elizabeth moved the boards," she said.

Before he could answer, I did. "Go ahead," I said to David. "We can put the plywood on top of these two-by-fours and it'll be easier because we'll be slightly higher.

Without answering he slowly got to his feet. He looked shaky, but I had to trust that he could do it. We'd have to get Suzie and Daisy over to the hole sometime, so why not now?

Before I started chopping I reached up and felt the roof. I was hoping my hand would feel more than my eyes could see. No such luck. There was more of a dent than a hole in the boards.

I drew back the hatchet and smashed it against the roof. It stopped dead against the wood and the vibrations shook down my arm. I drew it back farther and put my full force behind the blow. The hatchet sank slightly into the wood and I had to wiggle it back and forth to free the blade for the next assault.

David hadn't made much progress, but I was taller, and I had longer arms, and I was pretty sure I was stronger. I knew I could break through. I had to.

"Hold on a second," I said, and David paused before his next hatchet strike. We were switching back and forth repeatedly, whenever one of us got tired.

I reached up and with both hands grabbed the splintered remains of a board. I wiggled it back and forth and then twisted and pulled and it came free in my hands! I held it out, showing it off to David and Suzie as though I'd just won a prize.

Suzie didn't look over. She was just was staring at the water below, not moving . . . shaking from the cold. I wanted her to see that we were making progress, no matter how slow it was. I dropped the piece of wood and it splashed into the water, joining the rest of the flotsam of the McBrides' home.

I reached up again to see if I could free other pieces and my hand touched something soft—not wood. I pushed and it gave way. It was the shingle! We'd broken through the roof!

"Give me the hatchet!" I ordered.

I took it from David and pushed the blade against the shingle. It split open. I handed the hatchet back to David and grabbed the shingle, ripping it away. Immediately a little puff of fresh air came through the opening. I breathed it deeply into my lungs. It

Ici remplir week 3

was cool and fresh and moist, and so different from the stale air we'd been inhaling for the past few hours.

"Suzie, turn off the flashlight."

She didn't move. She didn't react.

"Suzie!" David yelled, his voice bouncing off the roof and startling Suzie back to attention. "Turn off the light! Now!"

Everything became dark, and then, not so dark. A shaft of light was coming in through the hole we'd created. Dim, growing wider as it fell from the roof, but it was light. More than that, it was a sign, a signal, a beacon—it meant that we just had to continue doing what we'd been doing, that it was possible, that we could chop through the roof. After working for what seemed like hours with no sign of success, this was like a shot of adrenaline. I knew we could do it. I'd give it one tremendous shot and I'd open that hole up wider. I figured this would be just like opening up a can—the hardest part was getting it started.

I drew my arm back and the blade of the hatchet slipped off the handle, bounced off one of the beams, and plopped into the water, instantly sinking out of view.

I stood there stunned, looking at the useless wooden handle in my hand. Then I looked at David, and back to the water where the blade had fallen, back to the handle, finally stopping at David again. My whole body began to shake and I started to cry. I had really believed we could do it, make it out, but now . . .

David jumped to his feet. For a split second I thought he was going to hit me because of what I'd done. Instead, he wrapped his arms around me.

"I'm so sorry!" I sobbed. "I didn't mean it . . . it just slipped off . . . it was an accident."

"It's okay."

"It's not okay . . . we need it . . . I'll go down and get it," I said.

That thought was terrifying—the blade would be almost eight feet under water . . . somewhere.

"No, you don't have to," David said.

"You're going to go?" I asked hopefully.

He pointed down at the two-by-fours. "We were studying medieval castles, and I read about how they used to break down those gigantic wooden doors. They used a battering ram."

He wiggled one of the two-by-fours out from under the edge of the platform, picked it up, and aimed it up at the roof. He drew it back and then slammed it against the roof. He did that a second time and then a third. On the third blow there was a loud crack and a piece of wood shot up into the air! The hole doubled in size!

"What if we both hold and swing it together?" I asked. Before he could answer one way or another I took hold of the two-by-four as well, putting one hand below and one hand above his.

"Ready?" David said. "On three. One . . . two . . . three!"

We swung the board up and it smashed into the roof with a tremendous crash, cracking another piece of the roof. The impact reverberated through my arms and right down to my legs, and it hurt my hands where they had slid forward. None of that mattered.

"Again!"

There was another crack, but this time the end of the board cracked as well.

"Turn it over," David said. We worked it around so that we had another new, solid side to ram with.

We hit it again, and again, and again, working into a rhythm. Some of the blows seemed to have no effect, while others caused cracks and crunches and chunks of wood to fly out or fall down.

"Hold on," I said, and I released my grip on the two-by-four. My hands were numb and sore and cut and bleeding, but I didn't care. I wiped them on my pants and reached up and grabbed the shingles that were hanging limply. I ripped off a big chunk and then a second. There was more light, and air, and rain. I could feel it on my face. It was still raining, but not heavily. The hole was so much bigger now . . . was it big enough?

"Give me a boost," I said.

David put down the two-by-four and clasped his hands together. I grabbed onto the rough edge of the roof, put up a foot into David's bridged hands, and then jumped. I bumped my shoulder against one side, but with David pushing from below and me pulling I popped out! I reached out and grabbed the television antenna, which was just above the hole. I used it to pull myself up and out until I was just sitting on the edge of the hole, my legs hanging down and inside.

"What do you see?" David demanded.

I'd been so focused on getting out that I hadn't looked any farther than the antenna. Mostly what I saw was water—foaming, boiling, bubbling, raging water everywhere. We were in the very middle of an angry river, and I couldn't even see the banks on either side. Just downstream there had been a line of big trees that marked the edge of the McBride property line. They were all gone, except for one large tree and a few smaller ones that had somehow managed to survive.

I leaned down so I could be heard. "We're in the middle of the river . . . I don't see shore in any direction . . . but it's dark . . . maybe it's just past the houses on the other side of the street. I'll look again."

I twisted around, holding on carefully, and peered into the distance again, hoping that maybe I would see something. Sticking out of the river were little islands, the houses of Raymore Drive. Trapped inside this house, I'd almost forgotten that we weren't the only house, the only people going through this. But where were those other people now? Had they gotten out before it was too late, or were they trapped in their houses still, or had they been caught by the current and swept away? I couldn't see anybody. I couldn't even see lights coming from any of the houses.

The sky above was dark, the stars and moon obscured by the thick clouds. The rain was still falling but it was just a drizzle. There were bursts of light—lightning? No, they were coming from the hills, from the edges of the valley. There were beams of light above the river. There were people up there looking down, trying to find us, find anybody caught in the river! If they could see us, at least people—our parents—would know that we were still alive.

I was below the peak of the roof. If I wanted to be seen—or if wanted to see what was on the other side of the house, the upstream part of the house—I'd have to scale the roof and get to the top.

"I'm going to try to climb to the peak," I called down to David.

"Wait, I'll come up and do it!"

"No, you need to stay with Suzie."

"Hurry, the water's almost at the platform now!" His voice had an edge of fear.

I felt the roof with my hand. It was cold and slick and, of course, wet. The rain wasn't falling hard but it was still dripping down from the shingles. I put one foot on the edge of the hole, and the jagged wood dug in through my soaked sock and into my foot. Bizarrely I thought about my new saddle shoes and wondered if they were still downstairs somewhere. I was better off without them right now anyway. I'd be better off without the socks, too—my feet certainly couldn't get much colder. I reached down and pulled off one sock and then the other. My bare feet would give me a better grip. I pushed off with one foot, pulled on the antenna, reached up to the very peak and tried to hoist myself up, sliding up a little and then slipping back down. The wet roof was as slick as ice. What would we hold on to? How could we all find footing out here? Now that we could get out to the roof, it was obvious that we should stay inside as long as possible. But how much longer was that?

I looked up at the peak again. Maybe if we could get to the top, to the peak, we could straddle it, with one leg on each side. That might work. I *had* to see if that was possible.

I dug my foot into the edge of the hole so I could stand up. Next I stepped up so that my other foot was wedged between the roof and the antenna. I pulled myself up, and then reached up and grabbed the peak. I pushed off, pulled, and prayed, and my head and shoulders and part of my body slipped over the top. I'd made it! I dug my toes in on one side and my fingers on the other. I threw one arm back and was able to grab the peak again and pull myself around. Now I was straddling the roof, riding it like a pony, but safely, securely sitting. I'd done it!

Right beside the McBrides' house was the Watson place—or at least that was where it *should* have been. It wasn't there. No, that couldn't be right. A house didn't just go away. Wait . . . the Watson's house was a bungalow. It wasn't gone, it was completely under water!

But what had happened to the Watsons? They hadn't driven out—that much I knew because I'd seen their car being carried down the river. Had they somehow managed to escape before the waters got too deep, before their house was submerged, or had they. . . ? I stopped myself from thinking any further.

I didn't know the name of the family that lived in the next house, but I knew them to see them. Their house sat looking like what I imagined ours looked like—a little peaked shadow rising out of the water. Wait . . . what was that on the roof? There was something on the roof, at the very peak. No, not something, *somebody!* Two or three figures were straddling the roof the same way I was. One of them started waving. They'd seen me! I waved my arms over my head and all three waved back wildly. I felt relief and a little rush of happiness. Not only were we not alone but I knew that at least some other people had survived. That was it, I had to get David and Suzie up here.

I waved goodbye to them and carefully slipped one leg back over the peak, keeping enough of my body over the other side to counterbalance. Slowly I lowered myself down, trying, and failing, to grip with my toes. I was extended as far as I could reach. Either I pulled myself back up or I let go. There was no choice. I slid down, reaching for the antenna with my hands and feeling for the hole with my feet. My toes jammed into the edge of the hole, but that didn't stop me! I slipped past the hole and I grabbed onto it with my arms and held on! Head first I clawed my way into the hole and—

"Elizabeth, you're okay!" David yelled. He reached up and grabbed my hands, pulling me farther in. I fell forward, into his arms and into water! Water . . . only a few inches deep. How could that be possible? Oh my God, the water had risen above the beams . . . we were standing on the platform but it was now beneath the water. Suzie threw her arms around me and started sobbing.

"We were calling and you weren't answering!" David screamed.

"I couldn't hear anything because of the noise of the river. I'm sorry!"

"We thought you were gone!"

"Gone? Where would I go?" Then I understood what he meant. They were afraid I'd been swept down the river.

"We have to get out," David said. "It's rising fast. Is there a place for us up there?"

"There is." I looked down at Daisy standing on the platform in the water, shivering and whining. There was a way for us, but was there for Daisy? She looked so woeful. I knew we couldn't just leave her here. We had to try to get her up and onto the roof. Maybe we could hold onto her.

"Give me a boost again. I'll go first. Then help Suzie up, and once I make sure she's safe, I'll come back and we'll move Daisy. You're last."

David didn't argue with my plan. He gave me a boost. It was much easier the second time. I pulled myself free and then spun around so I was hanging in the hole. I reached down and David was already holding Suzie up, her arms reaching toward me. I grabbed her by one wrist, my other hand holding the antenna. She was so light and so little that with David pushing and me pulling she came up with ease. I put her down on the edge of the hole, next to the antenna. She clung to my arm.

"You're going to go up there," I said. "To the peak. It'll be fine."

She nodded her head, wide-eyed.

"First you climb up to the antenna. I need you to put both feet right there."

She nodded her head. I held her hand and steadied her as she stepped up. She rested her second foot against the first, but she was fine there.

Next I lay down on the roof with my feet firmly on the edge of the hole so my body formed a ladder extending up past the antenna toward the roof.

"Climb on top of me, like a ladder, and get to the top!" I yelled.

She landed on top of me with a thud. Her hands wrapped tightly against my throat and her elbows and knees dug into me as her feet clawed for grip against my body.

"You're doing great, Suzie!" I yelled. I needed to encourage her. "Keep climbing!" I yelled, trying not to move.

She moved farther up until she was lying on the roof above me, her feet firmly on my shoulders.

"When you get to the top, throw one leg over the peak so you're riding the house!"

She reached up, and at the same time, I reached up with one hand and pushed against the sole of her foot, giving her a final boost. She reached the top and settled there, straddling the roof.

"Stay right there!" I yelled.

Now it was Daisy's turn. I slipped back down so my feet were dangling into the hole. I leaned into the hole and back into the house.

"Next comes the dog," I said.

"No, we don't have to. Not yet. Watch." David stepped off to the side—off the plywood platform and onto what had to be a rafter beneath the water. The little piece of plywood, with Daisy on top, wobbled and then started to float! "She's okay for a while. Let me come up and look first. I took the belt off my pants and made it into a leash for Daisy. See?"

He aimed the flashlight at Daisy. His belt was around her neck.

David tucked the flashlight into his pocket. The light was still shining, but it was almost all blocked by the material of his pants. He jumped up and grabbed the edge of the hole. I grabbed a handful of his shirt and helped pull him up and out. He got to his knees and then rose to his feet.

"The big trees are all gone!" he gasped, pointing downstream.

"No, there's still one." I turned around. The one big tree that had just been there was gone! In the few minutes that had passed, it had been swept away by the river. All that remained were the smaller trees, their top branches barely above the waves, but swaying and swinging and bouncing as the current hit against them.

"How could the little ones survive when the bigger, thicker trees were swept away?" David said. "That doesn't make any sense."

"No," I said, shaking my head. "The big trees couldn't bend. They stood against the current and tried to fight it. It broke them. The little trees don't fight. They bend and sway and let the current push them around. That's why they haven't been broken."

"I guess that makes sense," he said.

"But forget about the trees," I said. "Let's concentrate on getting up on the roof. Since you're up here you might as well go all the way to the peak."

"You should go first," David said.

"No, I'm taller and it's easier for me to reach. Besides, you're the one who's going to have to pull Daisy up once I get her out."

David grabbed the antenna, then he wedged his foot against it and pulled himself up to the peak.

He sat down, right in front of Suzie, facing toward her. She wrapped her arms around him in a big hug. She was cold and scared . . . we were all cold and scared.

I would have loved to join them up there, but I couldn't. I'd have to wait with Daisy, hoping the water didn't rise any higher. How many times had I hoped that and been disappointed? It was *going* to rise, and we'd *have* to get to the top of the roof. And where would we go from there? There was no place left to climb. We'd reached the top of the mountain and there was no more "up."

I suddenly felt a wave of exhaustion. I sat down on the edge of the hole. My feet were so numb I didn't realize that they were now half submerged. I looked down. Daisy was floating just beneath me. If I didn't bring her out right now the water would rise above the hole and she'd be trapped.

I reached down and grabbed the dog by the scruff of her neck and heaved her up. She was wet and heavy and struggled against me. I banged her against the roof and continued to pull until she popped out. Her claws scraped desperately against the shingle, getting no grip. What now?

I heaved her up so that her two front legs were on one side of the antenna and her two back legs on the other. I pushed against her with all my weight, pinning her in place against the roof. She continued to struggle and I pressed against her until she finally stopped.

I looked up. David was watching what was happening but he was helpless to do anything. I took the belt, the leash, in one hand and held it up, over my head. I was going to toss it up and hope he could grab the end. I threw it, and David reached out, but it wasn't long enough.

David lowered himself down. His legs were on the other side of the peak and he stretched, reaching out his arms toward me and Daisy. I threw the belt up and he caught it!

He began pulling and I pushed from below. Daisy struggled, unable to resist, but unable to help us, either. Her claws scraped uselessly against the shingles. David pulled and pulled and I pushed until she was above my outstretched arms. There was only a foot or so to go. David hauled her up farther and the belt suddenly snapped! Daisy slid down, right past me. I tried to grab her but she bounced off my fingertips and splashed down into the river! She disappeared from view under the water and then resurfaced a dozen feet away, facing us, desperately swimming, her paws digging into the water, trying to swim back toward the house, but being swept farther and farther away. Finally she disappeared into the darkness.

David once again had his arms wrapped around Suzie, and her face was buried in his chest. How awful. She had seen her dog, her Daisy, swept away down the river to certain death. David had his face down by her ear. Of course there was no way I could hear, but I knew he must be saying things to try to comfort her.

I climbed up, first to the antenna and then to the roof. I swung my leg over the peak and then dragged myself forward until I was sitting behind Suzie. I wrapped my arms around her from behind.

"Quit crying!" David yelled. "Stop being such a big baby!"

I was shocked. He wasn't comforting her, he was telling her off!

"There's nothing to cry about. The dog has four legs so she can swim twice as good as anybody else."

I thought about the dead cows and sheep I had seen, drowned, being pushed around in the current. He was wrong. Four legs hadn't helped them any. Daisy was as good as dead.

"She hates the water!" Suzie sobbed.

"That'll make her swim *harder* to get to shore. Stop blubbering like a baby!"

"David, she's scared and worried—"

"And you shut up too!" he barked. "The dog is fine. Understand?"

He shot me a look—not angry, but pleading—and instantly I understood what he was doing. As long as he was angry and difficult it meant that the dog was fine. He wasn't going to admit that there was anything worth crying about because the dog was *fine*.

"She's a springer spaniel," I said to Suzie. "Even if she hates the water she can swim really well. All springer spaniels can swim just fine."

"More than fine. Daisy can swim like a duck!" David declared. "Have either of you ever heard of a duck drowning?"

He had a point there. I almost believed him. I *wanted* to believe him.

"Right about now, that stupid dog is dragging herself out of the water, mad as can be because she had to get wet. She's going to shake herself off and then go find something to eat and a place to lie down and go to sleep!"

I could actually picture that whole scene in my mind.

"But how will we find her again?" Suzie demanded.

"The same way we found her when she got out of the yard last year," David said. "Somebody will turn her in to the pound and we'll go down and get her, or they'll even call us. She still has her collar and dog tag on. It was the belt that broke, not the collar." He was still holding on to the broken end of the belt and held it up to make his point.

"Enough about the stupid dog, okay?" he asked.

Suzie wiped her wet eyes with the wet sleeve of her sweater just as a beam of light swept from the hill and across the water right by where we sat. We all froze. It crossed over us for a split second, and the light practically blinded me.

"Maybe they saw us," David said excitedly. "Do you think they saw us?"

"If they had seen they would have kept the light shining on us instead of sweeping it away."

David nodded. He knew I was right. I felt bad taking away that glimmer of hope.

"They're aiming the light on the river."

"Why not at the houses?" he asked.

"Maybe they don't expect there to be anybody here any more. But there are. More than just us." I pointed at the house not far from ours.

With everything happening I'd forgotten about the people on the adjacent house. I looked hard. For a few fleeting seconds I couldn't see them and feared they'd fallen off and been swept away too. Then I saw a dark outline. They were hard to see. They looked more like a chimney than people . . . they *were* people, weren't they? I strained my eyes, trying to see through the darkness, through the rain—even the sound of the river seemed to make it harder to see—looking for any movement. I kept one arm around Suzie and waved the other above my head. They waved back!

"Do you see them?"

"I see them. That house belongs to the Van Dyke family," David said.

Suzie started waving wildly and yelling out "Hello!" There was no way they could have heard her over the roar of the river.

"How many of them are up there?" David asked.

"I think three."

"But there are five in the family. Three kids and the parents."

"Maybe a couple of them weren't home."

"Maybe it's the three kids, just like us," David said.

I hoped not. Somehow I wanted there to be an adult there with them, just like I wished there were an adult with us and I didn't have to be the one to make the decisions. So far none of those decisions had killed us, but none had saved us, either. David was right, if we'd just left in the beginning we'd all have been fine right now.

"Here comes the beam again!" David said.

The beam slowed down and changed directions repeatedly as different things were caught in the light. The river was filled with objects that had been picked up along the valley. We could see only the larger ones—tree branches, even tree trunks, garbage cans. And then, eerily, what looked like a whole barnyard full of pigs came into the spotlight. The light followed them as they popped up, twirled around, bounced and bobbed along.

It was as if they were in a race to see which could go fastest, which could get down the river first. I almost expected to see the Big Bad Wolf following behind them—but in an odd way I *was* seeing the Wolf, the river that had killed and devoured them. They rushed past the house, right down Raymore Drive, and for a brief second I thought the light might jump over and see us, but it never left the pigs. The light followed them as they raced down the river. They almost seemed alive, but of course they weren't—they couldn't be. I just hoped Suzie wouldn't think about them and then about Daisy.

"Did you see that?" David said.

"Of course, they practically bumped into the house."

"No, not the pigs, the Van Dyke house. No, forget it . . . it's nothing. My eyes are just playing tricks on me . . . I'm so tired," David said.

"We're all tired. What do you think you saw?"

"That house, the Van Dyke house, I thought it moved."

I jerked my head toward the house. It was still and standing and not moving. The three people were still silhouetted on the roof.

"There it goes again!" David yelled.

"It's just an illusion. It's not really moving, it's just the way the water is swirling around," I explained. "I always think the footbridge is moving when I look down through the chinks at the river."

"I saw it too," Suzie said.

"No, you probably just *thought* you saw it because David is talking about it. It's a house. It's solid. It won't move." It *couldn't* move. Houses didn't move.

"The river picked up cars," David said.

"A car is one thing. A house is another."

"And trees."

"Yeah, but still, a house is so much bigger and—" Then *I* saw it move. Or thought I did. I blinked hard a few times and rubbed my eyes. A house couldn't move. Could it?

"There it goes again!" David yelled.

"I saw it!" Suzie agreed. "It twisted!"

I gasped in horror. Cold, clammy terror filled my whole body. The house was spinning ever so slightly. It looked as though three of the corners had come loose, but the fourth was still holding it in place, and it was being turned, ever so slowly, on that one point. The side of the house slowly turned away from me until I began to see the front of it.

Then I stopped thinking about the house and remembered the people sitting on top of it. There were three of them, but from this angle I could see them only as one black mass. Then the spotlight came across the water and stopped right on the house, right on the people on the house! Under the bright, glaring light I could see them as clear as day. They were waving their hands in the air, frantically trying to signal the people on the other end of the spotlight. There was a man and two children—I knew the children. One was in high school now but had gone to my school before, and the other still went there, a few grades below me.

The girl, the older one, was in a nightgown, the boy just in his pyjama pants, and the man was wearing pants but no shirt. I pictured them as having been awoken from their sleep, the way we had been. Where were the mother and the other child? Now that I could see them I could picture the two who were missing. The mother often stood by the fence waiting for the kindergarten kids to be released, picking up her little boy. I'd seen her today . . . yesterday . . . it could have been a thousand days ago. The boy had been wearing big black rubber boots and a yellow slicker, probably a hand-me-down from his sister and he would have hated it. I'd seen them cross the footbridge ahead of us, so she must have been there to fix dinner for her family. But what then? Maybe she'd taken the little boy to her sister's house—she must have sisters—or they'd gone shopping and got caught and couldn't get back into the valley because the rain had already started falling so strongly.

Or maybe they had been swept away with the trees and the cars and cows and pigs and Daisy.

The house stopped spinning. Somehow it must have settled back down or—no . . . it wasn't spinning because it was now drifting . . . drifting toward us! The house, the whole house, brightly illuminated under the beam of the spotlight, was being pushed along by the force of the river! What would happen when it hit against our house? Would we stop it, or would it bump us and start us down the river as well?

Slowly, as if it were trying to sneak up on us, the house moved our way. First it would drift a few feet, then it would stop, then drift a few feet more. When the house came to a stop again it shuddered, as if it were afraid of what was going to come next. It looked as though it had been snagged or had hit against something or—the Watson house! It had come to rest against the little bungalow, hidden beneath the water.

The whole process was brightly lit as the beam of the spotlight shone directly on the house, directly on the three people on the roof. They were so close that I could clearly see their expressions, the looks of fear and confusion. The girl looked like she was crying—why shouldn't she? The only thing that had stopped me from breaking into tears a dozen times was that I knew I needed to look strong and calm and in control for Suzie.

Above the roar of the river I could hear them yelling, screaming, crying out for help. The whole scene was caught beneath the beam, focused one property over from us. If that beam would only shift, the people on the shore would see us, realize we were here. Even if they couldn't reach us, at least they'd know. At least our parents would know we were alive.

"It's moving again," David said.

I saw it too, but it wasn't moving toward us. Somehow it was sliding sideways. There was a scraping sound so loud that I could hear it over the rushing of the river. Then I realized what was happening. The current was pushing the house sideways. Because it couldn't go through the Watson bungalow, it was sliding along its side. And when it had been pushed far enough to one side, it would be free and go back to moving downstream.

The Van Dyke house began to turn again. The front of the house, the leading edge, was caught in the current while the trailing section was still sitting against the Watson house. Slowly it began to spin. Still spinning, the house moved right alongside us. The three figures, father and two children, were frozen in the glare of the spotlight. They were so close that I felt I could reach out and touch them, so close that I could talk to them. But even if my words could have been heard above the roar of the river what would I have said to them? Hello . . . I'm sorry . . . I wish I could help . . . goodbye. Goodbye.

The house gained speed. It started to buck and rock and bounce as it flowed faster and faster. The three figures were still caught in the glare of the spotlight, the white nightgown of the girl practically glowing. The beam of light was like a long, white leash, pulling the house forward, but also keeping it safe, stopping it from running away, so that they could just pull it to shore.

And then, despite the roar of the river, despite the growing distance between us and them, just before the house disappeared around a bend in the river, I thought I heard a scream.

David and I locked eyes over Suzie's head. His expression—fear, amazement, disbelief—mirrored my feelings. I wanted to say something, but my mind spun around and couldn't come up with words.

Suzie clung tightly to David. She was staring upstream to the place where the Van Dyke house had stood. She had seen a house—just like this one— get picked up and get carried downstream. She had seen three people—three like us—perched on that house get carried away. She had to have figured out their fate, what was awaiting them. She had to. She was only seven, but she wasn't stupid. Those three poor souls had probably been swept to their deaths. She had to know. How awful for them. How awful for us, having to witness it all.

Then I thought about something worse than just witnessing it . . . being next. My thoughts raced, trying to figure out how to explain to myself, to Suzie, to David why that house had been swept away and this house remained here. Was this house bigger, or built more solidly? Their house wasn't that much smaller or more flimsy than this one. Maybe it was one of the houses that had been built on stilts instead of on a foundation . . . no, I didn't think that was it . . . it had been on blocks on the ground, just like this one. There was no reason why it should have gone while we stayed. Why it should have gone while the rest of the houses on the street stayed . . . the rest of the houses.

I looked beyond where the Van Dyke house had stood. There should have been another house right beside it. Nothing. And then beyond that, nothing. There was a dark shadow, the outline of a house beyond that, but where three or four or even five houses should have stood there was nothing but dark, open space, filled with raging water. It wasn't just the Van Dyke house . . . it was a bunch of houses . . . four or five or maybe more.

Suzie suddenly began crying. I wrapped my arms around her tightly from behind. I needed to say something, but what? Was I going to tell her we were okay, that we were safe? What lie was I going to give her?

"I'm so cold," she sobbed.

"We're all cold," I said. I squeezed her even tighter, hoping the little warmth left in my body would help.

"We need that spotlight to come back," David said. "We need them to see us."

"It could be anywhere. This is a big valley with lots of houses."

"Do you think there are lots of people like us . . . lots of people trapped or missing or . . . ?"

He let the sentence trail off unfinished. Or *dead*. Or *drowned*. Lots. There had to be lots and lots.

This wasn't happening just on this street or even just on this river. Across the whole city, maybe even farther away, there had been flooding, and power failures, phones down, traffic accidents, and worse. So many people were scrambling just to deal with whatever was facing them, and any help available from police or fire departments would be spread out across the city. Why should they look here more than any other place?

"I just want them to see us. To know that we're here," David said.

"That would be good," I answered automatically, but then I thought about how little good that had done for the Van Dyke family. The light had allowed everybody to see their fate, but not change it. If I was going to die I didn't want it to be a public display. At least I wanted to die in private and not under the glare of a spotlight, like some circus performer who fell from the tightrope.

"If they saw us they could help," David said.

"What sort of help?"

"A boat. They could send a boat."

"Nobody would come out here in this river right now. Especially not at night."

"Somebody might. Somebody might be that brave."

"If they *knew* we were here and they came out, that would be brave," I said. "But to come out thinking that they *might* just happen to find somebody is just plain crazy."

"That's why the spotlight has to come back to see us."

"There are other lights."

The shore was alive, on both sides, with lights. Some looked like car headlights, and others, tiny ones, were probably flashlights, bouncing and bobbing and swinging back and forth. None of them seemed strong enough to penetrate the darkness as far as us. Only that big spotlight had come out this far.

"Wait a second," David said. "Maybe I can help them see us. I can shine the flashlight!" He reached into his pocket, pulled it out, and turned it on. The light was incredibly dim. I could barely see it. There was no way anybody on the shore would pick it out.

"It was a good idea," I said. "Might as well turn it off."

"At least the water isn't rising any more," David said.

"Are you sure?" I felt a spark of hope, the first I'd felt since the spotlight swept away from us. As long as it didn't rise we could just stay here and wait it out. It would be a long, cold, miserable night, but we'd survive . . . if the house survived. I tried to drive that thought out of my head. The house *would* survive.

"I've been watching. The water isn't rising any farther than the same spot on the shingles. It might even have gone down an inch or two. We'll just wait it out. When daylight comes, they'll be able to see us," David said, determinedly. "And then they'll send a boat . . . right?"

"They'll see us and they'll send a boat," I echoed.

I could sit up here all night and all day, I thought. I can sit up here as long as it takes.

I still had my arms around Suzie. She was securely sandwiched between us, and I thought maybe she had fallen asleep again. At least her eyes were closed. I felt so tired that I would have loved to close my eyes for just a few minutes, but I couldn't do that. I had to stay awake, try to stay alert.

"Did you feel that?" David asked.

I did feel it. "Something hit the house."

"Did you see anything?" he asked.

"I can't even see the house. Besides, lots of things are being pushed along under water. Probably more stuff is hitting us now that the Van Dyke house is gone."

"It's not just their house," he said. "Most of the street is gone." He paused. "I was wondering . . . why . . . why our house isn't gone."

"I guess this one is more solid." I still hadn't come up with a more convincing answer for myself.

The words had just escaped my mouth when I felt the whole house shudder.

"What was that?" It was Suzie. She had been jolted awake.

We all knew what it was. The house had moved. It was as if nobody wanted to say the words because if we didn't say them it couldn't be real. The whole house shook again and I felt it start to move, ever so slightly, but definitely. It shuddered and then stopped. It had moved only a foot, but it had moved.

Suzie started to cry.

"Shut up!" David yelled at her. "Crying doesn't help. We have to think!" This time he wasn't acting. He was really scared.

What good would thinking do? What was there to think about? How we were going to spin down the river like the other house? How we were going to die? Or else . . .

"We have to get off the house. We have to leave!" I yelled.

"Leave? Leave and go where?"

"The trees," I said. "We have to get to the trees."

There were five little trees just downstream, at the edge of the McBrides' property. They weren't far, two or three dozen feet. A short walk. A long swim.

"We have to be like those trees," I said. "We have to go with the current, let it push us into them."

"How do you know the current is even going that way?" David demanded.

"They're downstream."

"*Everything* is downstream!" he yelled. "Wait . . . let me check first."

He started to get up and I grabbed his arm. "No, you can't go in the water! Not yet!"

"Not me." He pulled off his sweater and scuttled forward, leaving Suzie and me behind. I kept my arms tightly around her.

"He'll be all right," I said to Suzie.

He stopped at the very end of the roof, held his sweater in the air, and then dropped it over the side. I caught sight of it, a dark shadow on the water, as it cleared the house. It was moving so fast, just racing along, and then it shot through a small gap between two trees. It had proved my theory . . . sort of. The sweater hadn't reached safety in the trees, it had kept going, down the river. There was nothing ahead except open water and darkness and danger . . . and death.

David motioned for us to come toward him.

"Just move slowly," I said to Suzie. Together as one, Suzie and I slid along the peak, keeping one leg on each side, until we reached David at the end. Beyond him was only a drop into the water. I wanted to go back to the centre where it felt safe. How strange that now *that* was what I considered safe.

I realized then that the house was starting to turn, slowly but definitely. It was starting to spin, the same way the Van Dyke house had spun before it was swept away. There was no safety in going back to the centre. There was no safety in staying where we were. The house was going to go, and we had to escape before it did.

"I'll go first," I said.

"Why you?"

"Just to see. You have to watch me . . . make sure that how I did it was right . . . and if it isn't, you have to try a different way . . . go into the water different. You and Suzie should go together. Hold onto her tight."

I took my arms away from Suzie and lifted one leg over the peak so I was sitting with both legs pointed down the slope of the roof toward the trees. The shingles were wet and I felt myself start to slide. I took a big breath and then closed my mouth as I plunged below the surface! The water hit me like a cold slap in the face.

I popped back up, opening my eyes and mouth wide as I groped for sight and breath. Instantly I was caught in the current and held, and I felt myself being pulled downstream. I tried to aim myself, move with the current toward the trees. A cross-current hit and I spun around, so I was facing the wrong way. I kicked my legs violently and spun back so I could see where I was going, so I could see the trees again. I grabbed for the branches at the same instant as my knees smashed against something under the surface. The branches slapped, stung, stabbed into my face. I grabbed on, clawing with both hands and scrambling with my feet, trying desperately to get some sort of grip. One foot caught and then the other and I clambered up the tree, the branches sagging and sinking under my weight. I kept climbing until my whole upper body was above the water. I had made it. I was safe!

Instantly I was hit with two urges—to simply freeze in place and hold onto the tree with both hands, and to climb up and out of the water completely.

I couldn't do either. I had to stay where I was, but I had to wedge myself in so I could use my hands to grab the others as they came toward me. I wrapped my legs firmly around the trunk.

I looked up at the house and didn't see their out-line on the peak. For a split second I panicked, and then I caught sight of motion. They slipped into the water, and my heart jumped into my throat. I was more afraid now than when I'd been in the water. They were right beside each other. The cur-rent caught them and they were coming right toward me!

"I'm here! I'll get you!" I screamed at the top of my lungs.

I could see them, see their faces. All I had to do was reach out and—

"I got you!" I yelled as I grabbed Suzie with one hand. My fingernails dug into her arm. I pulled hard, but the current was pulling even harder.

"Grab the tree!" I yelled.

Suzie reached out and took hold of a branch with one hand. David was holding on to her other arm—his grip on her was the only thing stopping him from being torn away and swept downstream. I reached out and over Suzie, grabbing for David, stretching, straining, trying to get to him. He reached out and grabbed my wrist. He pulled him-self up, clawing at my skin, pulling himself up my arm and then grabbing my top. For a split second I thought I felt myself start to slip off the tree. I tightened my legs around the trunk and he pulled himself forward until he'd climbed over me and into the branches.

I grabbed on to the tree with both hands now. I felt exhilarated, excited, exhausted. I wanted to yell, cry, scream, and laugh. Instead I just tried to calm my shaking limbs and reclaim my spent breath.

The next step was to get out of the freezing water. We were in little danger of being swept away now, but we were still in danger from the cold as long as our bodies were still mostly submerged.

"Suzie . . . you have to climb up."

She looked over her shoulder at me. She looked terrified. She didn't move.

"It's okay. I'm here. I'll catch you if you slip."

Slowly she began to climb up the tree until her legs were higher than my head.

"We have to get above the water . . . it's too cold . . . we can't survive in the water," David panted.

"We just have to climb higher, that's all."

I looked up at Suzie. There was space above her in the branches. If she climbed up higher we could follow.

"Suzie, climb up higher."

At first I thought she hadn't heard me, but then, slowly, she started to move. As she climbed the branches started to sag under her weight, so she really wasn't getting any higher.

"Now, you try to climb up," David said to me. "See if you can get out of the water."

"You . . . you should go instead."

"No," David said. "You first. I'll try too, but if I can't get above the water then we'll trade places after a while."

Part of me wanted to argue, but I was so cold that I knew I needed to get out of the water. I could feel it draining away all my remaining strength.

As I started to climb the branch started to sag, Suzie along with it. It was a balancing act. How much of me could I get clear of the water without causing her to be submerged?

My foot slipped off the branch and my knee hit against it. My leg was so numb that I didn't even feel it. There was no pain. Nothing. How long would I have to be above the water before I could feel my limbs again? Just as important, how long could David be down below with only his head and shoulders above the water?

There was a groan of creaking wood, so loud that it was audible over the roar of the river. The house had broken completely free of the foundation! It was slowing spinning, moving downstream . . . moving toward us! We had escaped the house, but now it was coming to reclaim us. We had to get out of the way, but there was no place to go. We were helpless, unable to move, right in its path.

In slow motion, the house rotated toward us, a massive dark shape, pushing an even darker shadow before it. The shadow engulfed us as the corner of the house hit against two of the trees—the trees right beside our little perch. The branches shook and snapped violently. The house pushed against them as it continued to rotate in the current. It spun away from our tree so that the whole side of the house hit against three of the other trees. The trees stood firm, holding the house in place, stopping the current from taking it away. For a second I had the crazy thought that we should just try to jump back onto the house now that the trees were holding it in place.

Almost in answer to my thoughts, the house started to move again. There was a tremendous scraping sound as the house pushed against the trees, snapped off branches, pushed them down under the water. Finally the house passed right over the trees, and branches popped back to the surface. Now free and in the current, the house raced away and was lost as it swept around the bend in the river.

The house was gone, but we were still here.

"Elizabeth, it's your turn, come on up!"

I looked up at David. He was above me in the branches of the tree. I heard the words, I understood what he meant, but I just couldn't make my body move.

"Come on, hurry up!" he yelled.

I stayed frozen in place. I just wanted to be left alone. I kept my eyes closed. I didn't want to open them. I was too tired, too bone-numbingly cold. I didn't know how much longer I could last. Maybe I could just keep my eyes closed, I could go to sleep, get away from everything, and when I woke up I would—

There was a hand shaking my shoulder roughly. My eyes popped open. David had climbed down and was in the water beside me.

"You have to get up into the tree. It's your turn," he said.

We'd taken shifts. Five minutes—or what we'd thought was five minutes—in the tree, and then five minutes in the water. Back and forth. We'd already traded four times . . . no, five times. How much longer could we do this? Not for hours. Not for another five minutes. I was finished. I was just going to stay where I was and go back to sleep. I closed my eyes again.

David grabbed one of my hands and yanked it from the grip I had on the branch. He reached my arm up to another spot.

"Take hold and climb up!" he yelled.

I tried to lift my leg. I couldn't feel anything, couldn't feel my foot, or my leg. It just felt heavy, tremendously heavy, as if it were made of lead. I couldn't lift it.

"I can't do it," I whimpered. "I can't."

"Elizabeth," David said softly. "You have to go on."

"I can't."

"You have to. We need you. Suzie needs you. Just go up and see her. Just try."

Suzie was in the branches over my head. She had her feet on the one solid branch and she was tied in place with what remained of David's broken belt.

"Just go and talk to Suzie," he urged me. "Let her know we're going to make it."

"We are?" I whispered. I wanted to believe him, but I couldn't. How could I? I wanted to give up, close my eyes, let go of the branches, and just be taken away.

"We *are* going to make it!" he yelled, and I was jolted awake again. "Now, go and tell Suzie. Go up there. She needs you!"

I couldn't give up. Even if I didn't believe it, I had to keep trying. Suzie needed that. I dragged my leg up and thumped my foot into a crook, pushing myself up. I did the same with my other foot, and now I was almost out of the water. I should have felt warmer but I didn't. The air was cold, and I started to shake all over.

"Suzie," I called out. "How are you doing?"

She didn't answer.

"Suzie?"

"I'm so cold," she whispered through chattering teeth. "So cold."

"You have to keep moving. Move your feet. You have to keep the blood flowing."

I wrapped both my legs and arms around the thin tree trunk. Anchored in place, my hands were free. I reached over and started to rub Suzie's legs.

"It hurts!" she cried.

"Then you do it."

"Both of you shut up!" David yelled. "Listen."

Listen for what? All I could hear was the constant rumble of the water as it streamed past us. Then, like a mirage, a little boat shot by, its motor whining, heading upstream. In it were two figures, two men! One was holding a big light, illuminating the way.

"Hey! We're here! Help! Help!" I yelled, but the boat and light went wide of us. It had passed so close, but they hadn't seen us.

I felt crushed. For a few brief seconds I had thought that maybe we were going to be helped, and then—the little boat started to turn, a little half-circle across the river, and then it was heading right back, not toward us, but downstream. I started to scream and wave an arm and David yelled and the boat jerked over to the side and came right at us!

The noise of the motor got louder and louder and then slowed down. The man at the front of the boat stood up, reached out, and grabbed hold of the branches. His hand was only a few feet from where I was holding on. I looked him straight in the eye, but I couldn't allow myself to believe that it was real, that *he* was real. This gigantic man was standing there, staring at me. And then he smiled—a gigantic smile. The beam of the flashlight came up and bathed me in light.

"Hold her steady, Herb!" he yelled over his shoulder. "Hold the boat steady!"

The beam of the flashlight bounced and then moved away from me. He'd dropped the light to his feet. Still holding on to the branches with one hand, he bent down, reached forward into the water, grabbed David by the arm, and pulled him up and out. He threw him into the boat like he'd just landed a fish!

The little boat swung around, as though it was trying to get free, but he held his grip, not letting it escape.

"You next!" he yelled at me.

I started to go and stopped. "No, her first! Her first!" I pointed at Suzie.

He looked up and his eyes widened. He obviously hadn't seen Suzie up in the branches above my head. All at once the whole world seemed to tilt to the side. The branches that were supporting me were pulled down, Suzie along with them. What was happening? Was the tree breaking? Were we going to be swept away at the last instant, just seconds before we were about to be saved? And then I realized what was going on. The man was standing up in the boat and he was pulling the branches down, pulling Suzie and me toward him. Lower and lower. Then, with his bare hands, he just snapped the branches off, and Suzie and part of the tree dropped into his arms. He lowered her into the boat, setting her down on the bottom beside David.

"Your turn," he called out.

I understood the words but for a few seconds they didn't make any sense.

"Yes . . . yes . . . I'm coming."

I released my grip on the branches and practically fell into the boat. The man caught me to soften the blow.

"Anybody else in that tree that I need to know about?" he asked.

"Just us."

"Get her moving, Herb!" he yelled. "You kids stay in the bottom. This is going to be a rocky ride." He let go of the branches and the motor roared as he gunned it and took us away from the trees.

"I'm Jim," he said, "and the guy back there is Herb."

"I'm Elizabeth Hardy, and these are David and Suzie McBride."

"How did you know we were there?" David asked. "Did somebody on shore see us?"

"Nope. I just caught sight of something in the tree as we passed by so I swung around to take another look," Herb explained.

"We've been out all night," Jim said. "This has to be our tenth or eleventh trip. We've found somebody every time. How long have you three been in that tree?"

"It seemed like forever," I said softly. Forever in a horrible dream.

The boat cut sharply in one direction so that I was tossed to the side, and I bounced along the bottom.

"Sorry about that," Herb said. "Telephone pole . . . I hate those telephone poles!"

"He has to keep cutting around things," Jim yelled out over the sound of the motor. "If we get hit by one of those poles the boat will be smashed to pieces."

"Darn poles are worse than the trees. They keep swishing by, passing like toothpicks!"

"Not that anything's going to happen," Jim said. "Herb here is a master at the helm of a boat! Nothing to worry about!"

"Just hang on tight," Herb said. "We'll have you to shore in just a minute."

I reached out and took Suzie's hand in one hand. I took David's in the other. They were huddled together on the bottom of the boat. I held them tight. I wasn't letting go.

I turned my head ever so slightly so I could see where we were going. From that angle, sitting at the bottom of the boat, I couldn't see the water any more. All I could see was Jim, perched in the bow, a small spotlight in his hands, lighting our route. Off to the side were the lights on the shore, little dancing lights, which were getting bigger and bigger and bigger. Then the motor got quieter and I could feel the boat slow down.

"Three more!" Jim yelled out. "Three kids!"

Jim jumped out and we were surrounded by people. Hands helped pull me to my feet and out of the boat. I was standing in knee-deep water. A blanket was wrapped around my shoulders, and there were voices, so many voices cheering and talking that I couldn't hear any of them.

David was helped to his feet and somebody picked Suzie up, wrapped a blanket around her, and started to walk away with her.

"Elizabeth!" she yelled. She began sobbing and screaming and struggling to get away from the man holding her. I broke free and ran, practically tripping and falling over my frozen feet.

"Here, give her to me!" I demanded.

"It's all right," the man said. "I've got her."

"No, give her to Elizabeth." It was David. He was at my side.

Reluctantly the man let me take her. Suzie stopped crying and wrapped her arms around me. David put an arm around my shoulders to help support me and Suzie.

I felt like laughing. I felt like crying. I felt like dropping to my knees and kissing the ground.

Those two men had saved our lives . . . and I hadn't even thanked them. I turned around just in time to see Jim push the boat off and he and Herb headed back out onto the river. I knew they'd been out many times already, but seeing them leave the safety of the land to go back out terrified me.

I wanted to run back, not just to thank them, but to tell them not to go, that they had to stay here, that they couldn't go. But then, I thought, what if somebody before us had convinced them not to go out again? What would have happened to us? What would happen to any people who were still stranded? I knew that they couldn't stop until they were sure there was nobody else out there.

I watched the boat spin around and turn back up the river. I watched until I could only see the spotlight plowing through the water, not the boat, or the brave men in it.

"Can somebody drive us to my house?" I asked. "I have to get home. I have to let my parents and the McBrides know . . . know that we're alive." Alive. We were *alive*.

"Sure, kid, no problem. You three can come with me." It was a policeman.

He started to lead us away. I staggered, and his hand steadied me before I could fall or drop Suzie.

"How about if I take her?" he offered.

"I can walk," Suzie said.

I put her down but kept her hand in mine. I wasn't letting go.

He led us to his police car and opened the back door. We all climbed in. The seat was soft and dry. It felt as unreal as being out on the river. He started the engine and we began to drive.

"I bet you three have quite the story to tell," he

"But we always knew we were going to make it," David said. He looked over at me. "We were safe as

On October 5, 1954, a major storm—Hurricane Hazel—started to develop off the coast of Grenada. It rumbled through the Caribbean and ultimately made land at North Carolina on the morning of October 15. It was expected that the winds and rain would dissipate, but instead Hazel regained strength and moisture as it crossed Lake Ontario. It became the largest storm ever to hit this far north: it had wind speeds of between 100 and 150 kilometres per hour and dumped close to 25 centimeters of rainfall in the Toronto area, causing massive flooding. Over four thousand people were left homeless, dozens of bridges were washed out, and eighty-one people died, including thirty-two on Raymore Drive, where all the houses on the lower part of the street were washed away.

For many years I had thought about writing a historical novel about Hurricane Hazel. I had even created an outline and thought of a title—*The Fury*. Then I came across a book by Steve Pitt called *Rain Tonight*. This wonderful book is a strange hybrid that is part picture book, part novel, part reference book. I called Steve to tell him how much I enjoyed his book—a book that should be in every library in the country. He graciously told me if I ever decided to pursue writing my novel that he would offer his assistance by providing the hundreds of pictures he had gathered, sharing stories, taking me for a tour of the site, and sharing the contacts that he had found in his research. His generous offer provided me with the impetus to take my original idea and create this novel. My personal thanks to Steve Pitt—a great writer, a generous soul, and a kind friend.

During the course of research I interviewed three people who were part of that amazing and terrifying night. Bryan Mitchell was a young man who was the acting Fire Chief for Etobicoke while his father was away at a convention. He supervised rescues, oversaw the damage, and lived through the tragedy of five volunteer firemen dying in the flood. He was then just a young man who shouldered this immense responsibility with determined professionalism.

Penny Doucette was in Grade 2 when she and her family chopped through the roof of their house on Fairglen Crescent to escape the flood waters of the Humber River. Her story is told in detail in Steve's book and is similar to the experience of the children in my novel.

Finally, there is Jim Crawford. Jim, along with Herb Jones, took a small motorboat out into the raging flood waters of the Humber. They dodged branches, trees, dead animals, cars, and floating houses as they repeatedly ventured into the river to rescue people. They plucked people from trees and roofs and brought them to safety. In the end, fifty-six people, including Penny and her family, were rescued by these two remarkable men who risked almost certain death to save lives.

Herb has since passed on. Jim is now a retired homicide detective with the Toronto Police Department. He is bowed with age, but he remains a bear of a man, large and powerful, and in his eyes you can still see the determination that marked his efforts that day. Rarely in life do you encounter a true hero. Jim is one, and it was an honour to meet him and have him share his story.

On October 15, 1954, I was only eight years old. I remember the day—lots of rain and a man walking me home under his umbrella to keep me dry. The ditches were overflowing with the amount of rain that had already come down.

Our home was right beside the Humber River—a house that my dad had built for his family. This was on Fairglen Crescent in Weston, Ontario. As a child, I loved living beside the river, as it was a real community in itself. All my fondest memories were swept away that terrifying night that Hazel came.

I remember listening that evening to my father talking to someone about how high the river was rising. Nothing to worry about though, as it had come up this much before. I fell asleep, only to be woken up in the middle of the night by my parents. We were unable to get out of our house; water was everywhere and now entering our house. My dad tried to reason as best he could, thinking he could maybe get to the maple tree outside, but upon attempting to do so he almost went under, as the step wasn't there anymore or maybe the house had lifted . . . who knows. That was a scary moment for me, seeing my dad in that situation and my mom trying to help get him back inside. I remember my father putting my two-year-old brother and myself on the kitchen table and telling me to pray.

An elderly neighbour was also with us at the time—she didn't want to be alone in the storm.

To get away from the rising water, all of us moved to the top of the stairs, near the attic. The front living room window crashed in with the force of the water. My mom was screaming for help—we had nowhere else to go. Then my dad found a hatchet and started to chop a hole in the roof to get us out.

He got us unto the roof through the hole he made. I remember water all along the eaves; there was just a roof in the middle of the water. My mom's screams brought some men in a boat and us children and my mom got in. Our elderly neighbour was still inside, and my dad resolved to stay and get her out through the hole in the roof. Later he had to hold onto a tree, persuading our elderly neighbour to persevere and hang on, too. Our house was swept down the Humber River just after my father got into that tree.

My father and my neighbour were rescued by those same two brave men in the boat who had rescued us—Herb Jones and James Crawford.

I will never in my life forget that night. We were all lucky to survive.

ERIC WALTERS, a former elementary-school teacher, began writing as a way to encourage his students to become more enthusiastic about literature. His many works include *Camp X*, *Royal Ransom*, and *Run*. His novels have won numerous awards including the Silver Birch, Blue Heron, Red Maple, Snow Willow, and Ruth Schwartz, and have received honours from the Canadian Library Association Book of the Year, and UNESCO's international award for Literature in Service of Tolerance. He lives in Mississauga, Ontario.

ALSO BY ERIC WALTERS
ALEXANDRIA OF AFRICA

For Alexandria Hyatt having a fabulous life is easy: she knows what she wants and she knows how to get it. Being glamorous and rich is simply what she was born to be. When Alexandria is arrested for shoplifting, having to drag herself into court to face a judge just seems like a major inconvenience. Alexandria has been in trouble before—but this time she can't find a way to scheme out of the consequences. Before she knows it, she is on a plane headed to Kenya where she has been ordered to work for an international charity.

Over 7,000 miles away from home with no hot water, no cell phone reception, no friends or family, Alexandria must face a land as unfamiliar as it is unsettling. Over the course of her month in Africa, Alexandria will deal with a reality she could never have imagined, and will have to look inside herself to see if she has what it takes to confront it.

Doubleday Canada / ISBN 978-0-385-66639-8